Additional acclaim for *Milkweed*

"*Milkweed* is fresh and vital. The writing is vivid and as funny as it is uncompromising in its depiction of the horrors of life for less-than-humans under the Jackboots. The banter between the street boys is especially strong—with childishness and high philosophy whisked together with the lightest of touches. The whole rings of authentic experience while also bearing the marks of a fine piece of storytelling."
—*The Guardian* (UK)

"Suspenseful . . . Spinelli's gripping narration will keep [readers] turning the pages."   —*Book Links*

"This is a superb addition to the canon of young adult literature."   —*Jewish Book World*

"Jerry Spinelli has fashioned a novel of beauty out of the ugliness of the Holocaust. It is a superb book, one of the best you will ever read."   —*BookPage*

"Unforgettable . . . a powerful story about one small boy's courage during a horrifying period of history. A heartbreaking and ultimately hopeful story."
—*The Midwest Book Review*

ALSO BY JERRY SPINELLI

Stargirl

Love, Stargirl

Crash

Knots in My Yo-yo String:
The Autobiography of a Kid

Today I Will: A Year of Quotes, Notes,
and Promises to Myself
(co-written with Eileen Spinelli)

JERRY SPINELLI

MILKWEED

A NOVEL

ALFRED A. KNOPF

NEW YORK

THIS IS A BORZOI BOOK PUBLISHED BY ALFRED A. KNOPF

Published in the United States by Alfred A. Knopf, an imprint of Random House Children's Books, a division of Random House, Inc., New York. Originally published in hardcover in the United States by Alfred A. Knopf in 2003.

Knopf, Borzoi Books, and the colophon are registered trademarks of Random House, Inc. Reader's Circle and the colophon are registered trademarks of Random House, Inc.

Visit us on the Web! www.randomhouse.com/teens

Educators and librarians, for a variety of teaching tools, visit us at
www.randomhouse.com/teachers

The Library of Congress has cataloged the hardcover edition of this work as follows:
Spinelli, Jerry.
Milkweed : a novel / Jerry Spinelli.
p. cm.
ISBN 978-0-375-81374-0 (trade) — ISBN 978-0-375-91374-7 (lib. bdg.)
ISBN 978-0-375-89037-6 (e-book)
[1. Boys—Fiction. 2. Jews—Poland—Fiction. 3. Warsaw (Poland)—Fiction. 4. Holocaust, Jewish (1939–1945)—Fiction. 5. World War, 1939–1945—Poland—Fiction.]
I. Title.
PS3569.P546 M55 2003
813'.54—dc21
2003040109

ISBN 978-0-375-86147-5 (tr. pbk.)

Printed in the United States of America
March 2010
10 9 8 7 6

First Trade Paperback Edition

Remembered:

Bill Bryzgornia
and
Masha Bruskina

ACKNOWLEDGMENTS

Many thanks to those who helped in the writing of this book:
Eileen Nechas, Patty Beaumont, Susan Cherner,
Charmaine Leibold, Laurie Baty, Ariel Gold,
Hildegard Veigel, Kathye Petrie, Eva Mercik,
Dr. Severin Hockberg, Rabbi Cynthia Kravitz,
Rahel Lerner, Chava Boylan, Jack Waintraub,
Marek Web, Peter Black, my editor, Joan Slattery,
and my wife, Eileen.

Smuggling was carried out through holes and cracks in the walls . . . and through all the hidden places unfamiliar to the conquerors' foreign eyes.

—February 26, 1941
Scroll of Agony:
The Warsaw Diary of
Chaim A. Kaplan

MILKWEED

1

MEMORY

I am running.

That's the first thing I remember. Running. I carry something, my arm curled around it, hugging it to my chest. Bread, of course. Someone is chasing me. "Stop! Thief!" I run. People. Shoulders. Shoes. "Stop! Thief!"

Sometimes it is a dream. Sometimes it is a memory in the middle of the day as I stir iced tea or wait for soup to heat. I never see who is chasing and calling me. I never stop long enough to eat the bread. When I awaken from dream or memory, my legs are tingling.

2

SUMMER

He was dragging me, running. He was much bigger. My feet skimmed over the ground. Sirens were screaming. His hair was red. We flew through streets and alleyways. There were thumping noises, like distant thunder. The people we bounced off didn't seem to notice us. The sirens were screaming like babies. At last we plunged into a dark hole.

"You're lucky," he said. "Soon it won't be ladies chasing you. It will be Jackboots."

"Jackboots?" I said.

"You'll see."

I wondered who the Jackboots were. Were unfooted boots running along the streets?

"Okay," he said, "hand it over."

"Hand what over?" I said.

He reached into my shirt and pulled out the loaf of bread. He broke it in half. He shoved one half at me and began to eat the other.

"You're lucky I didn't kill you," he said. "That lady you took this from, I was just getting ready to snatch it for myself."

"I'm lucky," I said.

He burped. "You're quick. You took it before I even knew

what happened. That lady was rich. Did you see the way she was dressed? She'll just buy ten more."

I ate my bread.

More thumping sounds in the distance. "What is that?" I asked him.

"Jackboot artillery," he said.

"What's artillery?"

"Big guns. Boom boom. They're shelling the city." He stared at me. "Who are you?"

I didn't understand the question.

"I'm Uri," he said. "What's your name?"

I gave him my name. "Stopthief."

3

He took me to meet the others. We were in a stable. The horses were there. Usually they would be out on the streets, but they were home now because the Jackboots were boombooming the city and it was too dangerous for horses. We sat in a stall near the legs of a sad-faced gray. The horse pooped. Two of the kids got up and went to the next stall, another horse. A moment later came the sound of water splashing on straw. The two came back. One of them said, "I'll take the poop."

"Where did you find him?" said a boy smoking a cigarette.

"Down by the river," said Uri. "He snatched a loaf from a rich lady coming out of the Bread Box."

Another boy said, "Why didn't you snatch it from him?" This one was smoking a cigar as long as his face.

Uri looked at me. "I don't know."

"He's a runt," someone said. "Look at him."

"Stand up," said someone else.

I looked at Uri. Uri flicked his finger. I stood.

"Go there," someone said. I felt a foot on my back, pushing me toward the horse.

"See," said the cigar smoker, "he doesn't even come halfway up to the horse's dumper."

A voice behind me squawked, "The horse could dump a new hat on him!"

Everyone, even Uri, howled with laughter. Explosions went off beyond the walls.

The boys who were not smoking were eating. In the corner of the stable was a pile as tall as me. There was bread in all shapes and sausages of all lengths and colors and fruits and candies. But only half of it was food. All sorts of other things glittered in the pile. I saw watches and combs and ladies' lipsticks and eyeglasses. I saw the thin flat face of a fox peering out.

"What's his name?" said someone.

Uri nodded at me. "Tell them your name."

"Stopthief," I said.

Someone crowed, "It speaks!"

Smoke burst from mouths as the boys laughed.

One boy did not laugh. He carried a cigarette behind each ear. "I think he's cuckoo."

Another boy got up and came over to me. He leaned down. He sniffed. He pinched his nose. "He smells." He blew smoke into my face.

"Look," someone called, "even the smoke can't stand him. It's turning green!"

They laughed.

The smoke blower backed off. "So, Stopthief, are you a smelly cuckoo?"

I didn't know what to say.

"He's stupid," said the unlaughing boy. "He'll get us in trouble."

"He's quick," said Uri. "And he's little."

"He's a runt."

"Runt is good," said Uri.

"Are you a Jew?" said the boy in my face.

"I don't know," I said.

He kicked my foot. "How can you not know? You're a Jew or you're not a Jew."

I shrugged.

"I told you, he's stupid," said the unlaugher.

"He's young," said Uri. "He's just a little kid."

"How old are you?" said the smoke blower.

"I don't know," I said.

The smoke blower threw up his hands. "Don't you know *anything?*"

"He's stupid."

"He's a stupid Jew."

"A *smelly* stupid Jew."

"A *tiny* smelly stupid Jew!"

More laughter. Each time they laughed, they threw food at each other and at the horse.

The smoke blower pressed my nose with the tip of his finger. "Can you do this?" He leaned back until he was facing the ceiling. He puffed on the cigarette until his cheeks, even his eyes, were bulging. His face looked like a balloon. It was grinning. I was sure he was going to destroy me with his faceful of smoke, but he didn't. He turned to the horse, lifted its tail, and blew a stream of silvery smoke at the horse's behind. The horse nickered.

Everyone howled. Even the unlaugher. Even me.

The pounding in the distance was like my heartbeat after running.

"He must be a Jew," someone said.

"What's a Jew?" I said.

6

"Answer the runt," someone said. "Tell him what a Jew is."

The unlaugher kicked ground straw at a boy who hadn't spoken. The boy had only one arm. "That's a Jew." He pointed to himself. "This is a Jew." He pointed to the others. "That's a Jew. That's a Jew. That's a Jew." He pointed to the horse. "That's a Jew." He fell to his knees and scrabbled in the straw near the horse flop. He found something. He held it out to me. It was a small brown insect. "This is a Jew. Look. *Look!*" He startled me. "A Jew is an animal. A Jew is a bug. A Jew is less than a bug." He threw the insect into the flop. "A Jew is *that*."

Others cheered and clapped.

"Yeah! Yeah!"

"I'm a horse turd!"

"I'm a goose turd!"

A boy pointed at me. "He's a Jew all right. Look at him. He's a Jew if I ever saw one."

"Yeah, he's in for it all right."

I looked at the boy who spoke. He was munching on a sausage. "What am I in for?" I said.

He snorted. "Strawberry babka."

"We're all in for it," said someone else. "We're in for it good."

"Speak for yourself," said the unlaugher. He came and stood before me. He reached down and fingered the yellow stone hung around my neck on a string. "What's this?" he said.

"I don't know," I said.

"Where did you get it?"

"I always had it."

He let go of the stone. He backed off to arm's length. He wet his finger with spit and rubbed my cheek. "He's a Gypsy."

There were gasps of wonder. The others leaned forward, munching, puffing their tobaccos.

"How do you know?"

"Look at his eyes. How black. And his skin. And this." He flicked the yellow stone.

The smoke blower said, "You're a Gypsy, ain't you?"

It sounded familiar. I had heard that word before, around me, in a room, near a wagon.

I nodded.

"Get him out of here," said the sausage muncher. "We don't need Gypsies. They're dirt."

The smoke blower laughed. "Look who's talking."

The one-armed boy spoke for the first time. "Next to Jews, they hate Gypsies the most."

"There's a difference," said another. "Everybody doesn't hate the Gypsies, but there's nobody that doesn't hate us. Nobody is hated close to us. They even hate us in Washington America."

"Because we boil babies and eat them for matzoh!" someone growled scarily.

Everyone laughed and threw food.

"We drink people's blood!"

"We suck their brains out through their noses with a straw!"

"Even *cannibals* hate us!"

"Even *monkeys* hate us!"

"Even *cockroaches* hate us!"

Words and laughter and bread and sausages flew through the

tobacco smoke and the horse's legs. Hands reached for the pile. Golden bracelets flew and jars of jam and tiny painted animals and fountain pens. The flanks of the horse flickered as they were pelted. A white-and-purple glass fish bounced off my forehead. The fox fur flew. One boy paraded wearing it about his shoulders, kissing its snout.

And then the stableman was coming and shouting and we were running, and outside we scattered like cockroaches and I ran with Uri and the thumping explosions were louder and the clouds in the sky were brown and black.

We ran through streets and alleyways to the back of a small brick building. Uri threw open a wooden hatch, and we plunged into a dark, cool cellar. Uri pulled down the hatch, snipping off the daylight, then he flipped a switch and a bare lightbulb burned among the cobwebs in the ceiling.

Uri pointed upward. "It's a barbershop. The barber went. He left everything. I'll show you tomorrow."

The cellar was a home. Carpets covered the floor. There was a bed and a chair and a radio and a chest of drawers. Even an icebox.

"Tonight you sleep on the floor," he said. "Tomorrow I'll get you a bed."

The explosions stopped, or maybe I just couldn't hear them anymore. We ate bread and jam and slices of salty meat.

I said, "What am I in for?"

He did not look at me. "You heard. Strawberry babka. Eat."

4

When I awoke the next morning, Uri was gone. He returned dragging a mattress. It was small, about half the size of his, but plenty big enough for me.

I lay down on it. He jerked me to my feet and snapped, "Not yet." He hauled me outside.

We walked to the shopping district, where the big stores were. Except some of them were not so big now; the bombardment had left them crumples of brick. Looking down the street, I saw spaces where stores should be. Like broken teeth.

We went behind the stores, to alleyways of trucks and trash bins and staring cats. Uri said, "Wait here." He disappeared in a maze of air shafts and fire escapes and doors, and when he came out his arms were loaded with clothes. "For you," he said.

I reached.

"Don't touch. Follow me."

He led me to a bombed-out building, nothing but the back wall standing. We climbed over a jumble of bricks and splintered wood and twisted pipe. "Watch the glass," he said. I kept stumbling over the heads and arms of manikins. We came to a lopped-off stairway. Uri tested it. "Okay," he said. We went down into the rubble. Whenever he came to a knob in a pipe, he turned it. Some gave out steam, some nothing. We stopped at one that gave water.

"Take those rags off," he said. I took off my clothes. He laid down the new ones and went rooting through the rubble. He returned with a manikin's leg and a scrub brush. He filled the leg with water. "I'm not thirsty," I said. He dumped the water over me. He began to scrub me with the brush.

At first it felt wonderful. Then it didn't. Leg after leg of water he poured over me. After the scrub brush got down to the soles of my feet, he started again on my face. He grunted as he scrubbed. I squirmed. I cried out. He was scrubbing my skin off.

At last he stopped. "Baby," he said. He dried me with a shirt. I screamed in pain from the rubbing. He patted the rest of me dry.

He glared at me. "Did you *ever* have a bath?" I stared at him. "Didn't think so."

Then he dressed me in a clean shirt and too-big pants. People gave us looks as we climbed out of the rubble and onto the sidewalk. By the time we were halfway home, I was feeling terrific. I felt new. I felt the air, the sun on my skin. Uri brought his nose to my neck and sniffed. He nodded.

Back in the cellar we ate sugar cookies and jars of plums in syrup. Then he led me upstairs to the barbershop. I had never been in a barbershop. He was right: the barber had left everything. Rows of colored liquid—green, red, blue—lined the shelf beneath a great mirror.

"You never had your hair cut, did you?" he said.

"No," I said.

"Have a seat."

I climbed into the red padded chair. He spun me around till I got dizzy. He pumped a lever and I rose higher. He shook out a large cloth and draped it over me. From a glass canister he pulled a comb and scissors and he began combing and snipping. Soon my hair was like fur.

"All right," he said, "which one?"

"Which one?" I echoed.

He pointed to the bottles. I did not understand why I should be offered a drink after having my hair cut, but I didn't argue. I had learned never to turn down food.

I pointed to the blue. "That one."

To my surprise he did not give me a drink but instead poured the blue liquid over my head. He shuffled his fingers through my hair and then combed it. It became wet and shiny.

Outside, people hurried this way and that. Many carried shovels.

"Are they going to a farm?" I said.

"They're digging trenches to stop the tanks," he said.

"What's a tank?"

"You'll see."

Soldiers marched and ran and blew whistles. People carried large fat bags. They must have been heavy, for one person could carry only one at a time, over his shoulders. If you had a wheelbarrow, you could take three.

"What's in the bags?" I said.

"Sand," he said.

I found out where the bags of sand went. I saw them stacked in front of machine guns in doorways and on roofs and at the ends of streets.

We hopped a streetcar as it rattled down the tracks. We got footholds on the outside and clung to window posts. The wind blew through my new hair. Passengers frowned at us. "Get off," they said.

"Look," said Uri.

A boy was running along the sidewalk at the same speed as us. It was the boy who blew smoke in my face. His arms were wrapped around a lamp of pure white glass in the shape of a naked woman. The lampshade fell off, but he kept running, weaving in and out of sidewalk people. I looked behind him. A man was chasing him, shouting, "Stop him!"

Uri swung out from the side of the streetcar like a gate. He waved. "Hey, Kuba!"

Kuba looked over as he ran. "Hey, Uri!"

It was then that someone stuck out a foot and tripped him. Kuba went sprawling, and the pure white naked woman shattered on the sidewalk. "Get him!" someone yelled, and the sidewalk people converged on Kuba.

"They won't get him," Uri said.

As the streetcar rattled on down the tracks, I saw someone swing a leg out and kick, and then Kuba was popping from the crowd and racing across the street, and the people hurled curses and laughter after him.

Uri shook his head grimly. "Stupid. Stupid. They take everything. Just to take it." He looked at me as the streetcar clanged above us. "Take only what you need. You hear?" He pinched my nose until my eyes watered.

I howled. "Yes!"

For a minute the passengers had forgotten us as they stared at the excitement on the sidewalk. Now they remembered us. A man in a silver necktie snarled, "Go. Get off." A little boy stuck out his tongue. And then a woman in a fox fur came down the aisle and reached over the seats and drew down the window on Uri's hands. I screamed, but Uri didn't. The fox's eyes were like little black marbles. The lady reached over to bring down my window too, but she stopped because there was a loud sound, and it wasn't the clang of the streetcar. It was sirens. Ahead of us a shop exploded in a gush of flame.

People screamed. The streetcar gasped and jerked to a halt. Within moments it was empty. Even the driver was gone, running with the crowds in the street.

And then the streets were empty. A strange music filled the air: the sirens' wail and the thump of exploding shells.

I pulled myself up into the streetcar. I opened the window that clamped Uri's fingers. He fell to the ground and in a moment appeared at the door. He threw his hands in the air and cheered, "Finally!"

I thought he was celebrating the release of his fingers, but it was something else. "I always wanted to drive one of these." He sat in the driver's seat. He stared at the controls. He pushed one thing, pulled another; the streetcar jerked into movement and we were heading down the tracks.

What a ride! Uri turned the steering stick this way and that. He learned how to make it go faster, then faster, and the street-car screamed along with us through the deserted city. Smoke rose beyond the rooftops, as if giants were puffing cigars. He showed me where to pull the clanger, and I pulled and pulled and the clanging joined the music of the bombardment.

At last we came to a loop, where the streetcar was meant to turn around, but Uri did not slow down, and the streetcar leaped from the tracks, and it was like riding a house into other houses. We smashed into a restaurant, plowed through a field of red tablecloths into the kitchen with an ear-ripping clatter, and still there were no people and no one to yell, "Stop! Stop!" Sauerkraut splattered across the windshield as we came to a halt against the ovens. By now the streetcar was on its side and we were hanging from our places. Uri was howling like a wolf, and even as the oven chimney pipes toppled like trees, I laughed and pulled and pulled the clanger rope.

5

AUTUMN

Soon the airplanes came, adding their waspy buzz to the music. I wanted to see them, but Uri would not let me go outside.

"Why can't we go out?" I said.

"They're dropping bombs," he said.

I thought: *This is what the enemy does. He flies overhead in his airplane. If he sees you in the street below, he reaches out and drops a bomb on your head.* I pictured bombs as black iron balls about the size of a sauerkraut kettle.

Every day the sirens screamed to tell us the bombs were coming. We stayed in the cellar and went out at night. That's when I learned the reality of bombs. Beyond the rooftops the city was on fire. It looked like the sun was stuck.

Those were the days and nights.

On some nights we were a city of two. We did not have to snatch. We simply walked into the empty shops of bakers and butchers and grocers and took whatever we pleased and walked out and walked home. We did not run. The streetlights were out.

Sometimes in the night we went to the stable. The others were there. Everyone put food into a big pile. We wrestled in the food before we ate it. We clubbed each other blindly with arm-long sausages. Cigarette tips glowed orange in the dark.

The horses were gone. The stableman never came shouting anymore.

Then one day the sirens were silent.

Uri and I were home, in our basement. Uri said, "Stay here," and went outside, and when he came back he said, "Let's go." He stuffed a cheese into his pocket and one into mine and we went up through the barbershop and into the street.

We walked fast. I could not keep up. Uri took my hand and pulled me. People were out. They were heading the way we were going. We passed the black, twisted skeletons of street-cars. Sometimes we had to trot down the middle of the street because the walls of buildings had crumpled and spilled over the sidewalks. Stacks of sandbags were everywhere.

People were hurrying. Machine guns looked to me like praying mantises. Airplanes flew overhead but no bombs fell from them.

I saw someone running. That was all I needed. I could not walk if someone else was running. I broke loose from Uri. Others were running. It was a race! I didn't know where the finish line was, but I was determined to win. Many had shouted, "Stop!" but no one had ever caught me. The street was getting more and more crowded as people poured into it. I streaked through the crowds. I passed other runners. I didn't care how many there were—I would beat them all. I laughed as I ran.

Then I was aware of a noise. I felt it before I heard it. It was deep and grumbling and seemed to come from beneath the streets. And there was another sound. It was like the beat of a great drum, or a thousand drums, and the more I ran, the

17

louder it became. And now the people were mobbed, piled like bombed bricks, the spaces between them gone, but I found spaces—I always found spaces—and I darted through them, I could taste the finish line, and suddenly I broke free, I burst out of the mob, I was in nothing but space and the drumbeat was deafening. "I won!" I shouted, and threw up my hands in victory. And then something hit me on the ear, and I was on the ground and the drumbeat was rolling over me. I looked up and I saw boots. The tallest, blackest, shiniest boots I had ever seen, endless columns. For an instant I saw my gaping face in one of them.

I knew what I must be seeing; Uri had spoken often of them. I gasped aloud: "Jackboots!"

They were magnificent. There were men attached to them, but it was as if the boots were wearing the men. They did not walk like ordinary footwear, the boots. When one stood at tall, stiff attention, the other swung straight out till it was so high I could have walked under it; only then did it return to earth and the other take off. A thousand of them swinging up as one, falling like the footstep of a single, thousand-footed giant. Leaves leaped.

The parade of Jackboots went on forever. Uri told me later that the street of the parade was so wonderfully wide it was not even called a street but a boulevard.

And then I was in the air. A hand had hoisted me up and I was dangling above the street and returned to my feet. A soldier was smiling down at me. His boots came to my shoulder, and his gray uniform was piped and spangled with silver. The brim of his hat was black and shiny like the boots; above it glistened a silver bird that I knew the boys in the stable would have loved to steal.

The soldier smiled down at me. He mussed my hair and pinched my cheek. "Tiny little Jew," he said. "Happy to see us, are you?"

"I'm not a Jew," I told him. I held up my yellow stone. "I'm a Gypsy."

My reply delighted him. "Ah, so, a Gypsy. Good! Very good!"

And he took me under both arms and lifted me and deposited me back on the sidewalk, at the front of the crowd. "Good day, little Gypsy," he said. And then the smile left his face and he stood tall and the heels of the boots snapped together with a *clack* and he saluted me and marched off.

The march of the Jackboots went on and on. After a while Uri found me. "Look," I said, "the Jackboots!" I thought he would cheer, but he did not. He stood behind me with his hands on my shoulders. I looked at the faces of the crowd. No one was cheering, or even smiling. I was surprised. Weren't they thrilled by the spectacle before them?

And now the deep grumbling was getting louder and beginning to overcome the drumbeat of the Jackboots. I had always looked to the sky for thunder, but this thunder was coming from beneath my feet. The street itself was trembling. And then I saw them. . . .

"Uri!" I cried.

"Tanks," he said.

Colossal gray long-snouted beetles—the tanks roared up the boulevard four by four and the sky shook on its hinges and I saw at once how silly it had been to try to stop them with ditches and sandbags and machine guns. I clamped my hands over my ears. A single white flower flew out of the crowd. It bounced from the iron flank of a tank and broke into petals. I had no flower, so I threw my cheese.

6

Uri and I walked outside the next morning to see how it was different. The tanks were gone. The Jackboots were strolling about just like us. They looked at the people and spoke to each other. I couldn't stop staring at them.

A crowd was running. We turned a corner. There was a large truck with the back open. Soldiers were tossing loaves of bread. The people grabbed and scrambled. We munched our cheeses, watching. I was fascinated. I had not known bread could be given.

We walked on. We came to another crowd of people, gathered around something on the sidewalk. "Don't," said Uri, but I did. I squeezed my way to the front. There was a man in a long black coat on his hands and knees. He had a long gray beard. Beside him was a bucket of water. He was dipping his beard into the water and scrubbing the sidewalk with the beard. A pair of Jackboot soldiers stood above him, laughing. Some of the people were laughing too. The man in black was not laughing.

I came back to Uri. I tugged on his arm. "Come see. There's a man cleaning the sidewalk with his beard!"

Uri smacked my head. "You *are* stupid." He pulled me away.

Farther on we saw something else that made us stop. Two soldiers were standing in front of another bearded man in black. One of the soldiers had a pair of scissors. He was cutting off the man's beard and the black hair that came curling down over his ears.

I ran up to the soldiers. "Bring him to our place," I said. "We live in a barbershop. He can sit in our red chair. We have bottles of hair tonic."

The soldiers stared at me. Uri grabbed me. He said words to them that I could not understand. The soldiers laughed. Uri yanked me away.

We heard the soldiers laughing behind us. I thought: *Men in beards and long black coats do not laugh.*

Later that day we sat on our beds eating chocolate babkas.

Uri said, "Stay away from Jackboots."

"They smile," I said.

"They hate you."

I laughed. "They don't hate me. They say, 'Very good, little Gypsy.' They salute me. I want to be a Jackboot."

He smacked me in the face. My babka went flying. "You're not a Jackboot. You'll never be a Jackboot. You are what you are."

I gathered up my babka. Still, I wanted to be right about something. "The people love the tanks," I said. "They ran to see them. They watched."

"They hate the tanks."

"Someone threw a flower."

He gave a snort. "Coward. If the Jackboots say, 'Kiss the tank's behind,' some people will do it."

I laughed, thinking of a tank's behind.

As I lay in bed that night, Uri's voice came through the darkness. "You need a name."

"I have one," I said.

"A real one."

"Why?" I doubted him.

"You should have one, that's all. I want to know what to call you."

"Call me stupid."

He laughed.

"You don't remember what your parents called you?"

"I don't remember parents."

We were silent. I moved my fingertip over my yellow stone. I remembered a booming laugh and bright colors. The smell of horse and the taste of something sweet. Riding someone's shoulder and hair glittering in firelight.

At last Uri's voice came again. "I had a little brother."

"Is he dead?" I said.

"Yes. I think so. He must be."

"Did he have a name?"

"Jozef."

"Was he little like me?"

"He was. And growing fast."

"Do you remember your parents?"

"Yes. But less and less."

I asked in the darkness, "Do you remember riding a shoulder?" but no answer came.

I closed my eyes and I thought over and over of Uri's words: *You are what you are.*

Which is what? I wondered.

In my mind I saw the man in black scrubbing the sidewalk with his beard. And the other man and the laughing soldiers with the scissors—*snip snip*—and the hair falling to the sidewalk, black hair falling . . .

My eyes popped open, though in the blackness there was nothing to see. "They're Jews!" I blurted.

Uri snorted. "Who says you're stupid?"

7

Those were the good times.

Our icebox, our cellar shelves, were full of food. We ate peaches in brandy and peanut butter and caviar sandwiches. We ate apples and lemon Danish and cheese puffs and hickory-smoked trout. We ate candy all day long. My favorite was buttercream with a hazelnut inside. There was usually only one to a candy box and often not even that, and I was not good at telling them on sight. So I broke open chocolates by the hundreds, searching for my prize. I raced through candy shops tossing boxes into a sack and raced out to the usual chorus of "Stop! Thief!" At home I frantically dug for hazelnut buttercreams, flinging the rest aside. Uri scolded me for wasting. Except for the candy, he made me finish eating everything I started.

As for Uri, he loved pickles. Big fat juicy pickles. They floated in barrels of brine in grocery stores. The urge would strike him suddenly. He would pop up: "Let's go. Pickle run."

We went on many pickle runs because Uri would eat only fresh pickles. If a pickle had been out of the brine more than a day, he stuck his nose up at it. This meant we had to keep finding new stores. No one ever saw him take anything, but after a while a grocer would begin to notice that whenever a certain red-haired boy came into the store, pickles disappeared.

On the way to a pickle place I was not allowed to snatch anything. Uri did not want his pickle run spoiled by a snatch-

and-run of mine. But on the way back, as he contentedly ate his prize, I was allowed to do as I wished.

Uri usually took things from store shelves and counters. Except for candy, I took from people. We would be strolling along, pickle juice from Uri's chin spattering the sidewalk, when I would see something and take it. Off I went, weaving through the crowds of people, while Uri munched away, pretending he didn't know me.

Back home, he would say, "How did you *do* that?"

I would shrug. "I just do it."

"You're amazing," he would say, and I would feel like a buttercream with a hazelnut heart.

Sometimes Uri went out alone. Scouting, he called it. He told me to stay put.

One time I did not stay put. It was not long after the Jackboots came. I got it into my head to go to the grand boulevard and see the parade again. That's what I believed: The parade was never-ending, it went on day and night. And I was missing it!

I climbed out of the cellar and started running. But when I came to the grand boulevard, there was no parade. There were streetcars and automobiles and people upon people, but no parade. I saw two Jackboots walking. I ran up to them. "Where is the parade?"

The tall one laughed. "You're five days late. It's over."

I tried to understand. "Are the tanks gone?"

"Not gone."

"Uri says you hate me," I told them, "but I don't believe him."

26

"Good."

"I want to be a Jackboot someday."

The tall one said something to the other, but I could not understand the words. He reached down and ran his fingers through my short hair. "Someday, dark little boy. Are you a Jew?"

"No," I said, "I'm a Gypsy. Are you a Jew?"

Again he smiled and said something to the other, who did not smile. "Let's hope not," he said, and they walked on.

I saw a lady carrying cream puffs. Don't ask me how I knew they were cream puffs. It was a white pastry box like any other, wrapped in white string. I just had a sense about those things. Maybe it came from snatching food for as long as I could remember.

I was coming up behind her. She wore a red coat, as the air was chilly. The seams of her stockings were perfect black lines running from her heels to the hem of the coat. Her blond hair spilled from a little black hat. The pastry box dangled from one hand.

She was not a screamer. Not everyone was. After I snatched the box, I heard no screams behind me. No footsteps either. She was not a chaser. Still, I ran. I always ran. I did not know how not to run. That was my life: I snatched, I ran, I ate.

So I was running, chased by myself you might say, and I turned a corner and was suddenly flat on my back. I had run into someone. A boy. With one arm.

"Gypsy!" he cried.

"My cream puffs!" I cried.

They were scattered about the sidewalk. So were his cherry turnovers. He reached for a cream puff and threw it at my face. I threw one at him. We laughed and scooped vanilla cream puff filling from our cheeks and ate it. We scooped vanilla filling and cherry goop from the sidewalk and what we didn't eat we flung at each other, and in between we fell onto our backs and laughed. Walkers veered into the street to avoid us.

"Well, well," came a voice. "Little thieves."

It was a Jackboot, grinning down at us—and we were gone, fast as flies, One-Arm one way, me another, the Jackboot's laughter fading.

I ran down alleyways. I didn't recognize where I was, but it didn't matter. I was in the city. The only world I knew.

I came to a garden. Some people had little gardens in their backyards. The gardens were all brown stalks and stubble and fallen leaves by now, and so was this one, except for one viny upshoot of green and red. It was a tomato plant, probably the last surviving one of the season. I knew something of seasons, but nothing of months and years—I had no use for them. I know now that this must have happened in the month of October in the year nineteen thirty-nine.

Many green tomatoes dangled from the vine, and two plump ripe red ones. I was still hungry. I pulled off a red tomato, sat myself down cross-legged on the ground, and ate it. The juice spilled down my chin as pickle juice often did on Uri. I picked off the other tomato. As I was eating it, I turned my eyes toward the back of the house. Someone was sitting on the step. A little girl. Watching me.

I never ate with someone watching me, unless it was Uri or

28

the boys. Eating came after running. And yet I didn't move. I sat there and ate the last red tomato in the city and I watched her watching me. Her elbows were on her knees and her face leaned into her cupped hands. Her hair was curly and the color of bread crust. Her eyes were brown as chestnuts. They were very big.

When I finished eating the tomato, I stood and walked off. I didn't run. When I looked back, she was still watching me. Her round, unblinking eyes made me feel as if I had just become visible, as if I had never been seen before. When I was far from the backyard, I kept looking back.

When I told Uri I found two red tomatoes and ate them, he didn't believe me.

On the first day that the light went out, Uri said to me, "Okay, this is who you are. Your name is Misha Pilsudski."

And he told me the rest . . .

I, Misha Pilsudski, was born a Gypsy somewhere in the land of Russia. My family, including two great-grandfathers and a great-great-grandmother who was one hundred and nine years old, traveled from place to place in seven wagons pulled by fourteen horses. There were nineteen more horses trailing the wagons, as my father was a horse trader. My mother told fortunes with cards. She could look at cards and tell you how you were going to die. She could look into your eyes and tell you the name of the person you would marry.

Every night the wagons stopped in a grove of trees by a stream. The chores of us little children were to gather sticks for the fire and to feed the horses. My favorite horse was a

29

speckled mare called Greta. Every night one of my brothers hoisted me onto Greta's back and I pretended to ride.

I had seven brothers and five sisters. I was not the youngest but I was the smallest. I was so small because I was once cursed by a tinker who did not like the fortune my mother gave him.

Since we were Gypsies we belonged everywhere, so we came to the land of Poland. My father traded many horses. My mother told many fortunes. Then we were bombed by a Jackboot airplane. The war had not started yet. Jackboot airplanes were simply flying about practicing for the war. The Jackboot general told the pilots that they could practice on Jews and Gypsies. So when a Jackboot pilot saw our seven wagons full of Gypsies, he immediately dropped his bombs on us, plus his goggles and everything in his pockets.

Fortunately, we looked up and saw everything coming down and we scattered—seven wagons in seven directions. I was with my mother and father. They were sad but I was not, because Greta, my favorite horse, was with us. Then one night, as we were camped in a grove of trees, some Polish farmers, who hated Gypsies even more than Jackboots hated Jews, came with torches and tied up my mother and father and stole me and Greta.

For a long time Greta and I were slaves for the farmers. They fed us nothing but turnips and pig's milk. Then one night Greta broke out of her stall and ran away. The next day I ran away too. I searched and searched for Greta and my family all over Poland. Finally, I came to the city of Warsaw, where I learned to steal food to keep from starving.

I never saw Greta or my parents or my brothers and sisters again.

And so, thanks to Uri, in a cellar beneath a barbershop somewhere in Warsaw, Poland, in autumn of the year nineteen thirty-nine, I was born, you might say. With one detail missing. I waggled my yellow stone in Uri's face. "What about this?"

He stared. "Yes . . . it was your father's. He gave it to you."

I was greedy. "What else?"

"Before you were kidnapped," he said. "That's all."

I loved my story. No sooner did I hear the words than I became my story. I loved myself. For days afterward, I did little else but stare into the barbershop mirror, fascinated by the face that stared back.

"Misha Pilsudski . . . ," I kept saying. "Misha Pilsudski . . . Misha Pilsudski . . ."

And then it was no longer enough to stare at myself and repeat my name to myself. I needed to tell someone else.

8

I returned to the backyard with the tomato patch and the little girl of the eyes. She was not there. Neither were the tomatoes. Even the smallest green ones were gone. But arrows were there. They were painted on pieces of paper, and the papers were pierced by twigs and the twigs were poked into the ground.

I followed the arrows. They led to a far corner of the garden. The last arrow pointed down. I dug with my fingers. I came to something. I pulled it from the dirt and brushed it off. It was the size of a walnut and it was wrapped in thin golden foil. I peeled off the foil. It was a piece of chocolate-covered candy. I broke it open. It was a cherry. Red juice spilled onto the ground. I ate it. I licked my fingers. It was no hazelnut buttercream, but it was close.

When I looked up, the little girl was on the step.

"Did you like it?" she said.

"Yes," I said. "But my favorites are buttercreams. With hazelnuts."

"I planted it in the spring," she said. "I planted a potato seed. It was supposed to be a potato. But nobody picked it when it was time to dig potatoes. Everybody missed it." She threw her arms out and shrugged to show that everybody missed it. "So it became candy. That's what happens when a potato stays in the ground too long. Did you know that?"

"No," I said. "My name is Misha Pilsudski. I'm a Gypsy from

the land of Russia. . . ." I held out my yellow stone. "My father gave me this before I was kidnapped." And I told her all about myself and my family.

She listened with her big eyes and her chin cupped in her hands. When I finished, she said, "It's not nice to steal. What are you looking at?"

"Your shoes," I said. I loved to look at them. They were black and as shiny as her eyes.

She held her leg out, turned her ankle this way and that. She held her foot in front of my face. "Look," she said. "See yourself."

I looked. There I was, as clearly as in the barbershop mirror. I looked . . . and looked . . . and then she was laughing. I was so intent on seeing myself that I hadn't noticed she was slowly lowering her foot; now it rested on the step and I was on my hands and knees, still looking.

We both laughed.

Then I said, "Are you a Jew?"

She made her mouth like a fish and drew in her breath. She put her finger to her lips and shook her head. She cupped her hands about my ear and whispered into it. "Yes. But I'm not supposed to tell anyone."

I said, "Does your father scrub the sidewalk with his beard?"

She frowned. "My father doesn't have a beard."

"Do you boil babies?"

"Of course not," she said. "What a stupid question."

"I'm a stupid boy," I said.

She cocked her head and stared at me. "How old are you?"

"I don't know." Uri had not told me that.

"I'm six," she said, "but I'll be seven tomorrow. I'm having a birthday party. Do you want to come?"

I said yes.

She jumped up from the step. She came and stood in front of me. She came very close until we were touching. "Stand straight," she said. I stood straight. I was looking at the back of her house through the brown curls on the top of her head.

Her hand appeared atop her head, mashing down the curls, moving forward until it touched the tip of my nose. She backed away.

"I come up to your nose," she said. "So you must be"—she stared at me, thinking; her finger pulled down her lower lip, showing her bottom teeth, one missing—"eight!"

She ran to the back door. She turned and pointed to me and said in a tiny, birdy voice, "Don't forget . . . party tomorrow." She went inside.

When I came the next day, she was standing on the step with her hands on her hips, glaring. Beneath a black velvety wrap peeked a pink dress that came to her knees. A red bow perched on her head like a little hat. She bent toward me, and I saw the red bow reflected in her shiny black shoes. "You're late."

"What's late?" I said.

"The party was supposed to start, but I told them it couldn't begin until you were here. Two of my friends already left."

With an angry grunt, she pulled me up the steps and into the house. She called out, "He's here!"

Footsteps from all directions, some running, some walking. We were in a room with a large table. On the table was food.

There were glass bowls of cookies and candies, but I could not take my eyes off the cake in the middle. I had never seen such a beautiful cake. It was a rectangle in shape, and it was a garden of frosting. There were frosting flowers of blue and yellow and green, and there was a little red frosting house with blue frosting smoke coming out of the chimney, and there was even a little frosting animal that looked somewhat like a dog but could have been a cat. Across the middle of the cake, in yellow frosting, something was written.

There were grown-ups around the table and three other little girls in bright dresses, who were giggling and staring at me. And then one of the women began to plant white candles into the cake. One candle went right through the red house. And then a man was leaning over with a lit match, and he put the match to each candle until all the candles were burning. I was shocked. They were going to burn down the cake! There wasn't a moment to spare. I blew out the fires, grabbed the cake, and ran from the house. Snow flurries swirled in my face.

When I told Uri what had happened, he laughed so hard he fell into his bed. I liked it when Uri laughed—his red hair seemed to brighten. He told me then about birthday cakes and candles, and I laughed also.

My running had caused the beautiful cake to crack like a bombed sidewalk. "Looks like we'll just have to eat it all ourselves," said Uri. Before we did, Uri read the writing across the cracks. He told me it said "Happy Birthday, Janina." I scooped up the writing with my finger and ate that first.

The next day I stole the best cake I could find from a bakery. I waited until dark and took it to the girl Janina's house. I set it on the back step. I took the candles from my pocket and planted them in the cake. I lit them with a match. I knocked on the back door and ran.

I wandered the city for the rest of the day. I did not head for home until after dark. Along the way I heard voices. I turned a corner. Fires burned in the night. My first thought was: *Someone is having an amazing birthday party.* But they were not candles, they were torches. Men were holding them in front of the same bakery where I had stolen the cake that day. Strudels and tortes danced in the firelight behind the glass. Someone painted a big yellow star on the window.

A man came out of a side door. He was in his stocking feet and held a coat about himself. At first no one saw him. He said, "Hey! What are you doing?"

The men with the torches and paintbrushes turned to him. They were glad to see him. They came to him. They took his coat from him. One of them held his arms from behind while another painted his face with the yellow paint that had made the star. The painter took great care to paint all of the man's beard. Then they took his clothes off. The man kicked and screamed. Someone put a torch near his face and he was still. In the torchlight, his eyes were fiery like the window of the bakery.

The painters painted the rest of him then, white and yellow from head to toe. They backed away and held the torches, the better to see him. The painted man looked like a very sad clown. The men with the torches and brushes howled with laughter. One of the painters reached out and paddled the rump of the painted man, setting off a new round of howls. Then someone snapped, "Go! Go!" and the painted man slumped back into his house.

It was then that I noticed flocks of torches up and down the street. Glass shattered. I turned another corner. It was everywhere: torches and laughter and shattering glass and painters painting windows.

I heard a horse coming. *Greta!* I thought, but it was not a speckled mare. Someone was riding the horse, but not in the usual way. He was tied to the horse stomach-down and backward. His bearded chin bobbed on the rump of the horse and his face went in and out of the horse's tail.

I thought: *I'm glad I'm not a Jew.*

As I walked home I looked up at the windows above the shops, where the people lived. All was dark and silent. Men in the street threw stones and broke windows, but still no faces appeared, no lights went on.

Early the next morning I dragged Uri out to see. People were still painting on the shopwindows, but this time the painters were the bearded people, the shop owners themselves.

I asked Uri, "What does it say?"

"It says, 'Jew.'"

"Don't they already know they're Jews?"

"They want everybody to know."

"Why?"

"So nobody will come to their shops and buy from them."

I thought for a minute.

"Uri, will you have to paint 'Jew' on the window of the barbershop?"

"No."

"But you're a Jew."

"In the first place, they don't even know I'm there. In the second place, who ever heard of a red-haired Jew?"

I thought some more.

"What about me? Will I have to paint 'Gypsy'?"

"No."

"Good," I said. But really, I wouldn't have minded so much painting "Gypsy" on the window. I even thought I might like having myself painted yellow and white from head to toe, especially if they let me keep my clothes on. What I really feared was being strapped to a horse backward with my face bouncing in and out of the horse's tail.

This time I said it out loud: "I'm glad I'm not a Jew."

Uri said, "Don't be too glad."

9

WINTER

They came in the night. I heard them above us. Shouts.
Laughter. Glass smashing. The hair tonic bottles! All the
beautiful colors.

Uri hauled me out of bed. "Coat! Coat!" I felt in the dark for
my coat. "Shoes!" I grabbed my shoes. He dragged me to the
hatch door that opened from the cellar to the backyard.

"Run!" he said when we got outside.

I wouldn't move. "My candy!"

He smacked me. We ran. Shouts behind us. Gunshots. The
yellow stone bouncing at my throat.

We ran for a long time, stopped to put on our shoes, ran. We
came to the jagged walls of a bombed-out building. We picked
our way through the rubble. Glass glittered in the moonlight.
Frost sparkled on tumbled bricks and fallen timbers. Uri took
my hand. We went down into the rubble.

Uri felt around, found a place. "Okay," he said, "sleep."

I slept. I dreamed I was standing underwater. A waterfall
maybe, or a faucet, splashing in my face, my eyes. I struggled to
breathe. I woke up. Above me, at the edge of the rubble, stood
a boy with schoolbooks strapped over his shoulder, blue sky
above him, a boy laughing, urinating in my face.

"Get out!" Uri shouted, and threw a brick. The boy vanished.

We went from that place to another, and another. We slept in many places. All were cold. Sometimes I awoke with snow in my ear. Never again did we sleep in beds, or sit in chairs, or reach into an icebox for food.

We walked the streets. Uri kept looking about. Sometimes he pulled me quickly into a doorway or a dark space between buildings. We did not go into any shop with a star on its window.

Whenever I heard a horse, I looked to see if it was Greta.

Uri had to go farther and farther to find pickles. He continued to find cans of meats and vegetables, jars of fruit and peanuts. He always took two of each. Candy he stole just for me. When I found a hazelnut buttercream, I could hardly chew it for laughing.

I used to see the brown paper bread bags everywhere I went. Now there were not so many.

One day when I snatched a loaf of bread, the lady called after me, "Stop! Dirty Jew!"

I stopped. I turned and faced her. I shouted back as sternly as I could. "I'm *not* a dirty Jew! I'm a Gypsy! My name is Misha Pilsudski!"

She threw her hands in the air. She called out to the people on the sidewalk. "A dirty Gypsy! Stop him!" She started running after me. The brown snout of her fox fur bounced up and down on her shoulder.

I had never gotten angry at a bread lady before. I turned the bag upside down and dumped the loaf to the ground. I jumped on it with both feet. I kicked it into the street. I laughed at the running lady and shouted, "Dirty bread lady!" and sped away.

The next day I stole five loaves. As I snatched each one, I shouted my name into the face of the person:

"Misha Pilsudski!"

"Misha Pilsudski!"

"Misha Pilsudski!"

"Misha Pilsudski!"

"Misha Pilsudski!"

"You cuckoo," said Uri when I got back. "It's too much. You're wasting." He took four of the loaves. "I'll give it to the orphans."

"What are orphans?" I said.

"Children without parents," he said.

"Like you?"

"Like me, like Kuba, like all of us."

"Except for me," I said. "I have a mother and father and seven brothers and five sisters."

"I forgot," he said. "Except for you."

We took the bread to the orphans. They lived in a large square house of gray stone. Uri rang the bell. The door opened.

Uri said, "Doctor Korczak, here is bread for the orphans."

The man looked at us. He was bald. The hair that was not on the top of his head seemed to have fallen to the bottom of his face, as he had a dense white mustache and a goatee like a broom. He smiled and nodded. "Thank you," he said. I peered into the dimness behind him, trying to catch sight of an orphan, but he was closing the door.

I had an idea. The next day I snatched two loaves of bread. One I gave to Uri, the other I took to the house of Janina the girl. It had snowed overnight. Brown stubble poked through

41

the white blanket covering the garden. I pushed the snow from the top step. I set the loaf down, knocked on the door, and ran.

The next day I came back to look. The bread was gone.

That was how it started.

10

From then on I tried to snatch two loaves each day. I would save one for Uri and me and leave the other on the back step of Janina's house. One time I looked up and saw her staring at me from the back window. She smiled. I smiled.

I began to find things on the step where I left the bread. I found a gumdrop and a candy cigarette and a fancy button. I always looked at the window, but she was never there again.

One day I left the bread and picked up a little black-and-white glass dog no bigger than my thumbnail. I was fascinated. I walked off, staring at the tiny dog, turning it over in my fingers. I was almost home—we were living in a stable loft then—when suddenly I turned and ran back to the house. It was in my mind to pound on the door, to make her come out so I could say something to her.

When I got there, someone was at the step. A boy. He turned and saw me. He stuffed the bread into his coat and ran. I ran after him, shouting, "Stop! Thief!" I caught up to him. I grabbed his long black coat, but he kept on running. He was a shoulder and head taller than me. I was his tail. I tripped and let go.

I ran after him again. We dodged in and out of people. They did not seem to notice us. Suddenly he turned. I ran into his fist. Next thing I knew I was in the gutter.

Pinpricks of frozen rain were falling. There was something hard in my mouth. I spit it out. It was a tooth. I reached into my pocket. The glass dog was smashed.

At home Uri's eyes bulged when he saw me. "What happened to you?"

I told him.

"You're too little to fight," he said. "You don't fight. You run."

He cleaned me up. He wiped blood from my face and ears and neck. When he touched my face, it hurt. He kept muttering, "Stupid . . . stupid . . ."

Next time I wasn't stupid. I went at night. There was no one on the streets. I wondered where the people were. The streetlights were like moons cupped in iron fingers.

Behind Janina's house there was no light at all. I ran my hand across the step. I felt something. I put it in my pocket. I put the bread on the step. I looked up at the window, but it was even darker than the night. Somewhere in the house Janina was sleeping. I waved at the dark, empty window and went away.

Back on the street, I heard a shout. I turned. Someone stood up the street, in shadow. He stepped into the light. I heard a pop, saw a flash, felt a tug on my ear. I reached up. I couldn't feel my earlobe. Someone was shooting at me! I ducked into the nearest air shaft and made my way home along the alleyways.

My ear hurt. I cried. Uri came to me. When I told him what had happened, he flicked his cigarette lighter to see. He smacked me and stuffed a rag against my ear. "Stupid . . . stupid . . ."

"I can't find my earlobe," I told him.

"They shot it off," he said.

"Who?"

"The Jackboots, who do you think?"

"Why did the Jackboots shoot my ear?"

"Because of the curfew."

"What's the curfew," I said.

He turned off the cigarette lighter. He was a voice in the black. "Curfew means all Jews off the streets after dark."

"But I'm *not* a Jew."

"If they shoot at you, you're a Jew. I told you not to go out at night. You don't listen." He flicked on the lighter, smacked me again, and flicked off the lighter.

It was true. He had told me. It was also true that I didn't listen. I had sneaked out while he slept. To show him I understood, I smacked myself.

Before I went to sleep I remembered my pocket. I pulled out the thing I had found on Janina's step. Feeling it, I could tell it was a hair bow. I guessed it was red, the one she had worn on her birthday. I put it in a bread bag, where I kept all the things she left on the step.

The next day Uri tied a rope around my wrist. "Teach you a lesson," he said. We went off to meet the boys.

We met them in a cemetery. They laughed when they saw me.

"He's on a leash!"

"Bowwow!"

"Toss him a bone!"

"Look—he was in a fight with another dog. It bit his ear off!"

45

"Let him alone," Uri said.

"Let me alone," I said. "I have seven brothers and five sisters."

They laughed even louder, but they left me alone.

There was smoke-blowing Ferdi and Olek with one arm and grim-faced Enos and the rest of them, but there was no pile of treasures anymore and there were no cigars and no one threw food about. But there were cigarettes—Ferdi pulled a handful from his pocket—and everyone lit up, even me. It was my first cigarette.

"He's smoking!" exclaimed Kuba, who was a clown.

"He'll stunt his growth!"

"How can he? He's already smaller than a cockroach!"

And then Kuba the clown charged into one-armed Olek. The two of them wrestled, but it was no match. Olek was much better with two legs than Kuba with two arms. Olek had Kuba wrapped like an octopus, Kuba squealing and flailing. Kuba grabbed Ferdi's leg and bit it. Ferdi screamed, and in a moment everyone but Uri and grim-faced Enos was on the ground, even me with my leash. We laughed and bit and wrestled, and I think we must have looked like one squirming creature with many heads, arms, and legs.

At last we peeled apart and flopped to the ground, exhausted and laughing. My ear was bleeding again and hurting. I pressed a fistful of dry grass to it.

Except for Kuba, we sat on the ground and talked and laughed and smoked our cigarettes. But that didn't last long, as the frozen ground was even colder than the air. One by one we stood. We milled about. We bumped into each other and grappled. We made a game of giving and receiving bear hugs. To see who is strongest, we said, but I think it was to be close. In the cemetery our bodies were the only fires.

Some of us played hide-and-seek among the tombstones. I was It, and when I went seeking I came upon a tombstone such as I had never seen before. Rising up from a great block of stone was a man with wings. He was looking at the sky, as if he might fly off at any moment. I couldn't take my eyes away.

"Hey, Gypsy," came a voice, "come on, we're hiding."

But I just stood there staring up at the great stone man with wings. Soon others were standing by.

"Who is he?" I said.

"It's an angel," said Ferdi.

"What's an angel?" I said.

Grim-faced Enos said, "There are no angels."

I looked at him. I pointed to the man with wings. "So what is that?"

"Just stone," he said. "It's not real. It's something Jackboots believe."

"I believe," said Olek. He scratched the stump of his missing arm. "There *are* angels. You just can't see them."

"Why not?" I said. "Are they hiding?"

"They're invisible."

I looked around. I had to agree: if they were there, they were invisible all right. Which made it especially good to have a stone statue of one. At least I could see that.

"What do they do?" I said.

"They don't do horseflop," said Enos.

"They help people," said Olek. "When you're in trouble, they help you out of it."

47

Enos snorted. He ground out his cigarette on the foot of the stone angel. "Where were they when you got pushed to the tracks and the train ran over your arm?" He grabbed the empty sleeve of Olek's missing arm and flapped it in his face. "Where were your angels then? Why didn't they roll you off the tracks? Why didn't they stop the train?" He pointed at a boy called Big Henryk. His shoes were bank coin bags. "Look at him. Why don't the angels give him shoes? Or brains to want them? And him"—jabbing his finger at Jon, who was thin and gray and never spoke—"look at him. He's dying and he doesn't even know it!" Enos was shouting now. "What are your *angels* doing for him?" He spit on the stone angel.

All was silent . . . until the cry "Jews!" came skimming over the tombstones.

We turned to look. A black wagon was coming down the path. The lumbering horse wore a black shawl over its mane. A line of people, black-shawled and lumbering like the horse, followed the wagon. It was a small wagon, a cart, just big enough to hold the coffin.

A man was shaking his fist. "Jews! Hooligan Jew-boys filthing up the cemetery!"

Several of the men left the line and headed toward us, shouting. We flung our cigarettes and ran. My leash flapped wildly, slapping tombstones. Suddenly Kuba stopped. He turned his back to the men, dropped his pants, and bent over and gave them a good, long look. The running men shouted louder, but no louder than we laughed.

*　　*　　*

48

In the stable that night, in the straw-smelling darkness, I said to Uri, "Is Enos right? There are no angels?" There was no answer. "Are you sleeping?"

"I'm trying to," came his voice. "Your silly questions. How do I know? Enos is whatever you want him to be. You want him to be right?"

"No," I said. "I want him to be wrong."

"Fine. He's wrong."

"I want to believe in angels. I think."

"Fine. Believe."

"But Enos says angels are for Jackboots."

"You're a jack*ass*, that's what you are. And a silly one."

"You don't say I'm stupid anymore. Now I'm silly."

"Take your pick."

"But I'm not a Jackboot. How can I believe in angels?"

"When you're nothing, you're free to believe anything. Go to sleep, Misha."

I tried to go to sleep, but a question kept nagging me.

"Uri?"

He snarled, *"What?"*

"Do *you* believe in angels?"

"I believe in bread," he said. "Now shut up or I'll come over there."

I shut up.

11

As if heeding Uri's words, bread soon became something more to believe in than to eat.

One day I went to my usual spots. Street corners near bakeries—these were the best. I waited at the first. No one came along with a bread bag. In fact, no one even came out of the bakery. I went to the next spot. Same thing. All day I went from corner to corner. Nothing. Not a single loaf of bread did I see.

I did something I almost never did—I entered a bakery. It was a bakery with a yellow star painted on the window. I was shocked. On the shelves against the wall there was no bread at all, only a single, sad round roll. Behind the glass in the case were two or three cupcakes.

The baker came from the back room. "You want to buy something?" he growled.

I stared at the roll. It was better than nothing. But it was too high for me to reach. My speed and quickness were useless.

I showed him my yellow stone. "Trade?" I said. I would not have given it to him. I just wanted to trick him into taking down the roll.

His face turned red. He jabbed at the door. "Out! Get out of here, you little thief!" He reached for me, but I was gone.

Back in the stable I said to Uri, "There's no more bread."

"Learn to eat pickles," he said.

I did. I learned to eat a lot of things. If there was no food on the streets, under the arms of the ladies in the fox-face furs, I went to the shops. If the shelves of the shops were bare, I went to the homes. There was always food in the homes, especially the large, fine houses, the houses that the ladies of the fox-face furs went back to.

I had to be patient. It was hard to find an unlocked door. I learned to look for little children playing outside a large, fine house. When they went back inside, they often forgot to lock the door. In I walked, sometimes right behind the child. Some children looked back at me and said, "Who are you?" "Misha Pilsudski," I said. Some children said nothing. They seemed to think that if I strolled in the door with them, I must belong.

I walked straight to the dining room or the kitchen. What happened then depended on who and where the people were. If there were only children, I might say, "Where are the cookies?" or "Where is the candy?" If there were grown-ups about, I grabbed the first thing I saw and ran. If there was no one or a very young child, I would take my time shopping in the kitchen.

One time I entered a house through an unlocked back door. I heard voices and laughter. I moved through the kitchen and suddenly found myself standing in a doorway, staring at a family of people having dinner around a long table. Food and silver and glass sparkled everywhere. In the middle was a great, golden roasted bird, perhaps a goose or turkey. I must have surprised them, for all movement stopped as they stared at me while I stared at the table—but not for long. As always, I was the first to move. I believe this was the first rule of life that I learned, though it was a twitch in my muscles rather than a thought in my head: *Always be the first to move.* As long as that happened, they would have to catch up, and I could not be caught.

I snatched the bird by the leg and bolted from the back door before they were out of their seats.

Of course, I could not do this more than once at any one house, but there were many large, fine houses in Warsaw.

Uri tied me to his own wrist when we went to sleep, so I could not deliver food to Janina in the night. During the day I left things on the back step—a jar of jam, a drumstick—but I could never be sure they were not stolen.

When the bread started to go, so did the trees.

I heard them going early one morning. I felt the night leash tug on my wrist. I joined Uri at the window of the loft. Outside, men were standing knee-deep in snow, chopping down trees.

"Why are they chopping trees?" I said.

"Firewood," he said. "People are running out of coal. They're cold."

Wherever we went looking for food, we heard the sounds of hatchets and saws. And trees. Some trees fell with an almost silent *whump* into the pillow of snow. Some gave a groan. Some shrieked in protest. One, a thick, burly monster of a tree with warts, came down with a high, thin wail that sounded exactly like a baby crying.

Soon the parks were nothing but dry grass and stumps.

One day Uri went off by himself and came back with a sack of coal. "Black pearls," he said. He took the black pearls to Doctor Korczak, to keep the orphans warm.

The next day I too went searching for black pearls. I scrounged deep into the rubble of collapsed buildings, tunneling for coal bins. I found a piece here, a piece there, but it was mostly coal dust. When my sack was finally full, I marched to the orphanage and rapped with the brass knocker.

An orphan boy came to the door. His mouth dropped open, his eyes bulged when he saw me. I blurted, "I'm not an orphan! I have seven brothers and five sisters!" I held out the sack. He ran.

In a moment Doctor Korczak appeared. Again I held out the sack. "Black pearls," I said. "Keep you warm."

His great white mustache stretched in both directions, and he laughed. "You"—he pointed at me—"are the black pearl." He disappeared from the doorway. He returned with a mirror. "Look."

A face black as coal itself stared back at me. I never knew eyes were so white. I looked at the rest of me, my hands, my clothes. I was a walking lump of coal. "I'm black," I said.

He laughed again. "Not for long." He took the sack of coal and led me into the house.

He waved his arm. "Welcome to our wonderful home."

Soon I was in something called a bathtub and a lady on her knees was scrubbing me with a brush and soap, and as I became white again and my stone became yellow again, the water became as black as Jackboots.

In distant rooms I heard laughter and the sound of running feet. I felt orphan eyes on me, but I could not see anyone.

Doctor Korczak brought me new clothes, the second person

ever to do that. As I put them on, he said, "So, little sack of warmth, I think you are a Gypsy. Am I right?"

"Yes," I told him. "I used to be stupid, but now I'm silly."

He laughed. He laughed a lot. "Who told you that?"

"Uri," I said. "Uri is my friend. Do you believe in angels?"

He stopped laughing. He stared at me. "Yes, I do believe in angels."

"So do I," I said, deciding once and for all. "Uri believes in bread."

He nodded. "Yes, I believe in bread too." He was always smiling. His mustache made it seem a double smile. "What is your name, little man?"

"Misha Pilsudski," I said proudly.

His eyebrows went up. "Ah! Yes." He nodded and closed his eyes. *He's heard of me*, I thought. "Misha Pilsudski . . ." He seemed to be tasting my name. "Tell me, Misha Pilsudski, where do you live?"

"In the stable," I said. "With Uri. But the horses are gone."

"And tell me, do you happen to be an orphan, Misha Pilsudski?"

I loved his goatee even more than his mustache. It was so soft and white. I wanted to rub my face in it. I wanted to climb inside it and live there and peek out. I think he wanted me to be an orphan very badly. I hated to disappoint him. "Oh no," I said. "I have seven brothers and five sisters. And a mother and father and a great-*great*-grandmother who's one hundred and nine years old and a horse named Greta if I can ever find her." I told him how we had been bombed by Jackboots and the whole story.

Then Doctor Korczak left me waiting for a few minutes. When he returned, he led me to the great front room. I was amazed. There they were, the orphans, orphan boys and orphan girls, all of them standing at attention in rows from wall to wall.

Doctor Korczak snapped his fingers and everyone said at once: "Thank you, Misha Pilsudski!"

I was uncomfortable. I didn't know what to say. Doctor Korczak shook my hand and opened the front door for me. "Come see us again," he said. I walked away in my new clothes.

12

I continued to bring black pearls to Doctor Korczak and the orphans. To Janina's back step I brought black pearls and bread when I could. I began to notice that there was no longer a gift waiting for me. One day I knocked on the back door. A man answered. I knew he was a Jackboot even in his socks. His gray-and-silver jacket was unbuttoned, showing a stained T-shirt and suspenders. In one hand was a stein of beer.

"Where is Janina and her family?" I said.

He growled something at me in Jackboot language. His breath was oniony.

I repeated forcefully: "Janina!"

He took a swig of beer. He pointed at the bag of coal in my hand. I held it out. "Black pearls," I said. "For Janina." He snatched them from me.

He pointed at me. "Jude?"

That word I knew. "No," I said. "I'm a Gypsy."

He cocked his head, as if to hear better.

I stood at attention. "Gypsy!"

He raised his hand. I thought: *He's going to salute me.* But he didn't. He slapped me. And overturned the stein of beer onto my head.

I snatched the bag of coal back from him. I swung the bag and brought it down with all my might onto his stockinged foot. He yowled. I ran.

* * *

One morning after awakening in our stable, as I was walking to the stall where we peed, I saw a man in another stall.

He was curled up like a bean. He wore a long black coat. He lay in the straw. I squatted down beside him. Suddenly one eye opened and stared at me. He sat up.

"Do you live here?" I said.

Straw poked from his head like extra hair. "I live nowhere," he said.

"I live here with my friend Uri," I told him. "Do you want to live with us?"

He looked around as if there was something he could not find. He shrugged. "Maybe."

"Did you once live in a big house?" I said. I was thinking of Janina.

"The house was big," he said, "but I only lived in two rooms."

"With your children?"

He looked at me. "With my books."

I studied his face. "You're not a Jew, are you?" I said.

His eyes shifted. He sat up straighter. "Why do you ask?"

"You don't have a beard."

He stood. He peered into the next stable. "That's because I'm not Jewish. Did someone tell you to ask?"

"No."

He repeated, "I am not a Jew. Do you believe me?"

"Yes," I said. "I'm not a Jew either. I'm a Gypsy. I'm glad I'm not a Jew."

He walked to the nearest window and looked out. "Glad, are you?"

57

"I think so," I said. "But sometimes I'm not sure. Jews get shot at and they have to ride horses backward and scrub the sidewalk with their beards. But I don't have a beard. And I think I might like to get painted."

He was looking at me, but he didn't seem to see me.

"Would you like some bratwurst?" I said. "We have bratwurst."

I waited. At last he nodded.

I went for the bratwurst. When I returned, the man was gone.

When Uri and I walked the streets, I had strict instructions. I was to walk as if I knew where I was going. I was to look straight ahead. I was not to laugh or scream or dance or do anything to call attention to myself.

"Be invisible," he said.

"Like an angel?" I said.

He ignored me. He said I was to look as if I had nothing to hide, as if I belonged there. "Most of all," Uri said, poking me in the chest, "don't look guilty."

"What's guilty?" I said.

"It's doing something you're not supposed to do."

"That's easy," I said. "I'm *not* guilty." I had forgotten about snatching Janina's birthday cake.

"Fine," he said. "Just don't look it."

I found a scrap of mirror. I looked into it. I practiced looking not guilty. I walked back and forth in the stable, looking straight ahead, looking as if I had nothing to hide. When we went outside, in the center of the city among the crowds of people, I said to Uri, "Look!" and crossed the street by myself. I held my head high. I looked straight ahead. I looked as not guilty as anyone ever looked and as if I knew exactly where I was going. I got hit by an automobile.

It was only a bump. The car screeched and stopped and hit me just hard enough to knock me off my feet. The driver was screaming, people were staring, and next thing I knew Uri was dragging me by the collar of my coat and at the same time kicking me in the rear and the people were laughing.

Uri wasn't laughing. He dragged me out of sight into an alley and dropped me like a sack of coal. He hissed in my face: "Did I tell you not to call attention to yourself, you stupid little turd?"

I looked up at him. I nodded. Back to stupid.

I had never seen him so mad. His hair looked redder than ever, only this time it was not because he was laughing. He punched me in the forehead. The back of my head banged against the wall. "Someday I'm going to have to kill you to keep you alive." He flapped his arm. "You want to do it your way? You want to go off by yourself? Not listen to me? Go ahead!" He kicked me. "Go ahead!" He stomped off. By the time he reached the street, I was at his side.

I was sure then that I would never again disobey Uri. But I did not know about the beautiful horses.

13

The first time I saw it was the time Uri first took me to the orphans' home. It was in a park within sight of the home. I couldn't believe my eyes: horses going in a circle. I thought they were real. Then I saw they were not. They were made of wood, painted, going round and round to tootling music. I ran to them. I just stood there, overwhelmed. They were the most magnificent animals I had ever seen—red horses, blue horses, horses of all colors—draped in gold and flowers, heads high, hooves raised as if prancing to the music. I barely noticed the children sitting on their backs.

"What is it?" I said to Uri.

"Merry-go-round," he said.

The horses went round and round. As each wonderful horse went by, its large black eye seemed to look straight at me. So proud and high were their heads, I saw for the first time how miserable were the real horses plodding the streets. Some of the children bounced and yelled, pretending to gallop. Others looked thoughtful. One was crying. Grown-ups stood watching.

Someone pulled the crying child from her horse. I headed for it. Uri grabbed me. "No."

"Why?" I said. I tried to pull away.

"It's not for you."

I thought he was joking. "Everything is for me!" I said, laughing. I believed it.

He grabbed my neck in one hand. He squeezed until I couldn't breathe. He brought his face close to mine, his pickle breath. *"No."*

We turned our backs on the merry-go-round and went to the orphans' home.

From then on I went to sleep with the tootling music in my head. Gold-spangled horses circled my dreams. By morning there was only straw in my ears.

Whenever we went out together, I tried to steer Uri toward the merry-go-round. As we came near, I could always feel his hand slipping over my collar.

I'm sure he knew I disobeyed him when I went out by myself. Many days I headed straight for the beautiful horses. But they were not always moving. "Electricity," Uri had once said, explaining why our lightbulb used to work only sometimes when we lived like kings in the cellar of the barbershop. "It comes and goes."

So it was an even grander treat to see the horses moving. I couldn't resist. The first day I went back alone I was determined to ride a horse. There was a foot of snow on the ground, but I never felt the cold. Every gilded saddle was occupied. I stood watching them go round and round. I think my eyes must have been as big as the horses', my smile as wide as those of all the laughing children put together.

And then the horses slowed down and came to a stop, and the music stopped, and the waiting people rushed forward and pulled the children from the saddles. I didn't wait. I leaped onto the platform and onto a horse. It was the most beautiful of all the beautiful horses, and I had had my eye on it from the start. It was as black as the coal dust under my fingernails. It had gold tassels behind its ears and a flying tail and three golden hooves on the ground and one in the air. Its head was flung high and its mouth was open as if shouting to the horses of the world: *Look at me!* For those few moments I was higher, I was grander, than anyone.

Then a child was screeching, "He doesn't have a ticket!" and a man came along and held out his hand and said, "Give me your ticket," and I said, "What's a ticket?" and the man yanked me from the horse and threw me facedown into the snow.

Within moments a little girl with hair as gold as the horse's tassels stood above me pointing and screaming, "He's a dirty Jew!"

I got to my feet. Everyone was staring at me, even the foxes on the shoulders of the ladies. I screamed back at her. "I am not!" I screamed at them all. "I'm a Gypsy!"

"Eewwww!" The golden-haired girl held her nose and kicked me and ran off shrieking. Other children tugged on the hands of the ladies, like dogs on leashes. They flung their faces at me. "Dirty Gypsy! Dirty Gypsy!" One by one the little girls were let go. They dashed forward, kicked me, and dashed back to the laughing ladies. Meanwhile, the boys bombarded me with snowballs.

I ran.

But I returned the next day, and the next. When the horses were moving, I stayed at a distance, watching, wishing.

One time when I brought coal to the nearby orphanage, I said to Doctor Korczak, "Do the orphans ride the merry-go-round?" Sometimes I saw the orphans play outside, but never near the merry-go-round.

Something sad came over Doctor Korczak's face. "No," he said. "Maybe someday."

I looked up at his round face, at the fabulous white goatee. "Why not?" I said. "Because they're Jews?"

He looked at the merry-go-round tootling behind me. He looked at the orphans playing nearby. Girls were jumping rope. He smiled at them, such a smile as I imagined must come from fathers. "They're *children*," he said. He sounded surprised. He looked down at me. *"Children."* There was a question on his face, but I could not answer it.

This thing electricity, I did not understand it. It came and went without warning. I marveled that without it, lights were dark, the merry-go-round was still. For two or three days the painted horses had not moved. I imagined I heard them screaming, *Let us run!*

Then in the dark of the stable one night, I awoke to the sound of the music. Often in the night I heard the music. Uri explained that the music was only in my head, for the merry-go-round was two kilometers away. And besides, the merry-go-round did not turn at night.

But this time it was different. The music was not in my head, I was sure of it. I went to the window. A full moon falling on the snow lit up the world—who needed electricity? And somewhere out there music was playing. Uri slept. I sneaked out of the stable—Uri no longer tied me to himself—and into the curfew.

The music got louder and louder as I came near the merry-go-round. I was right! I started to run. The snow slowed me down. And there it was! Lit up by lights that I had barely noticed in the daytime. The music was tootling, the horses were going round and round, the lights were blazing—and no one was there! The mysterious electricity must have come on in the night and awakened the merry-go-round.

I climbed onto the beautiful black horse with the golden tassels and round and round we went. I went from horse to horse until I think I must have ridden them all. I rode them forward and backward. I rode them sitting down and standing up. I don't think I ever stopped laughing, and in the mix of my laughter and the music I was sure I heard the whinnies of the horses, joyful to be moving again.

And then a thought came to me. I stopped laughing. I looked at the dark hulk of the orphans' home. I jumped down from the merry-go-round. I wobbled and fell into the snow, dizzy from hours of riding in circles. I ran to the orphanage. I banged on the door. I called out, "Doctor Korczak! Doctor Korczak!" A light went on inside. Locks clacked. He opened the door. Fear was in his eyes.

"Doctor Korczak!" I blurted. "The merry-go-round is going! Look! There's no one there! Bring the children!" I took a step back. I waved. "Come on!"

The doctor reached into the moonlight and hauled me roughly into the house. He slammed the door shut and bolted it. He shook me by the shoulders. He snapped, "Foolish, good-hearted boy." He hauled me upstairs to a bed.

As I went to sleep in the orphans' home, the moon was

going, morning was coming, and day was darker than night. When I awoke, Uri was downstairs whispering with the doctor. Their cloud-breaths mingled.

As we left the orphans' home, I waited for Uri to smack me, to knock my head into a wall, to call me stupid. He did nothing. He said nothing. As we walked through the snow, I looked up at him. If only he would squeeze my neck, make me cry. He did not even look at me. Then and there I lost my desire to ride the beautiful horses.

But not to look.

14

As the winter went on, the trees around the merry-go-round disappeared one by one, until soon there was nothing but stumps. And then the unthinkable happened.

I was approaching the merry-go-round one day when I noticed that things were different. A great crowd was gathered around the platform, but there was no music, no movement. As I wormed my way through the crowd, I heard someone cry out, "A Jew did it!" I wondered what it could be that a Jew did. Then I saw. I couldn't believe my eyes: one of the horses was gone!

Only three hooves remained. I had come to think of the horses as so real that for a moment I was surprised to see blond, splintered wood instead of blood and bone where the legs had been chopped off. A scrap of surviving color told me the horse had been black. It was mine. My beautiful black-and-golden horse.

"Find the Jew!" people were calling. As I stared at the three horseless hooves, I felt my own anger rising. "Find the dirty Jew!" the voices called over and over, and I think one of the voices I heard was mine.

At the edge of the park two Jackboots stood talking and smoking cigarettes.

They found the Jew. Or should I say, they found *a* Jew. Jews were interchangeable. One was as good as another. I was to learn this many times. So, before the morning was over a Jew came stumbling through the snow with a rope around his neck. He was led out to a clearing among the tree stumps. Someone noosed another rope around his neck. Someone else ripped off all his clothes. Until that moment I had not noticed how cold it was.

The man seemed to shrink, seemed to pucker into himself until all there was was bulging eyes. The snow covered his ankles.

"Make way! Make way!" someone growled. Two Jackboots hauled a fat black hose through the crowd. They stopped ten meters from the shrinking man of eyes and pointed the hose at him. Water leaped out. The hose flew out of the Jackboots' hands and whipped wildly about like a sliced worm. People screamed and ran. The Jackboots jumped onto the hose head and wrangled it down. They hugged it to themselves and again pointed it at the man. When the water struck him, he flew backward. The two ropes around his neck jerked him to a halt. The hose men backed off some more.

Things settled down then, and the people gathered again. Some cheered and laughed and clapped. Some merely watched. I didn't think it was possible, but the man's eyes got even bigger. I could tell he was trying to shrink even more, to vanish completely. He never made a sound. When I walked away, he was turning blue.

I did not return to the merry-go-round until the snow was gone and the grass was greening among the stumps. I wondered if the man had melted away like the snow. The three hooves were gone from the platform. The only reminder of what had happened was the empty space where the beautiful black horse had been. Otherwise all was as always: the music was tootling, the ladies were laughing, the children were going round and round. . . .

15

AUTUMN

The people were going. I had never seen so many people walking. We were standing on a street corner, watching.

They were Jews. I knew by the armbands they wore. Every Jew had to wear a white armband with a blue star. This was a big help in telling who was a Jew, as they no longer wore beards. Until that moment, I had seen only a few Jews here, a few Jews there. I had not known there were so many.

They came from many places, many streets, but they were all going in the same direction. Little children pulled wagons heaped high with toys and pots and books. Grown-ups pulled wobbling carts of furniture and clothes and pictures and rugs. It seemed they had emptied their entire houses into wagons and carts and the bulging sacks over their shoulders. Larger wagons were pulled by horses, smaller carts by people. The horses and the people looked alike, plodding, eyes to the ground, leaning forward against the weight of their loads. The horses did not wear armbands, yet they too were clearly Jewish.

It was a blue-and-white parade—and how different from the grand parade of the Jackboots! So slow, so quiet, hardly a baby cried. The thump of a thousand Jackboots was now the shuffle of ragged shoes; instead of the roar of tanks, the crickety click of cart wheels.

I shaded my eyes. "Where are they going?" I said to Uri.

"The ghetto," he said.

"What's the ghetto?"

"Where the damned live."

Though the people were quiet, there was much noise behind them. There was whistling and cheering and breaking glass. As the moving people came down out of their houses, other people rushed in. There were fistfights in the courtyards. People sailed from doorsteps. Top-floor windows flew open, the new house people shouted over the heads of the walkers, "It's mine!"

But I was more interested in this ghetto place, wherever it was. "Be back by curfew." It was all the warning Uri gave me anymore.

I walked with the Jews. For a while I got carried away. Ever since the great Jackboot parade, I had wanted to be in one. And so I marched along in a parade of my imagination, passing one plodding Jew after another, head high, arms swinging, goose-stepping as if I wore tall shiny boots myself. If anyone noticed, I was not aware. No one said a word. Soon enough, my imagination petered out and I slowed down to the pace of the others.

I found myself walking beside a boy who looked Uri's age. The boy hauled a gray sack that bulged as if it held pumpkins.

"Do you know Uri?" I said.

The boy kept staring straight ahead.

I repeated myself, louder. "Do you know Uri?"

The boy did not seem to know I was there. That didn't stop me. I was determined to talk.

"Uri has red hair. He's not a Jew." I was always careful not to give Uri away. "Can I touch your armband?" He didn't respond. I touched it. "I'm a Gypsy," I told him. "Maybe some-day I'll get an armband too."

I pulled a sausage from my pocket. (I carried a sausage with me whenever I could find one. I snacked on it through the day.) I held it up to him. "Would you like a bite of my sausage?" For the first time I saw his eyes move. Then the lady walking on the other side of him said, "He's not hungry. Please go."

That was ungrateful, I thought, but I did as she said. I went from person to person, asking questions: "Are you going to the ghetto? . . . Will you have a nice house in the ghetto? . . . How much farther to the ghetto?" I never received an answer. To one and all I offered my sausage, but no one took a bite. No one saw me, or so I believed—except the foxes on the shoul-ders of some of the ladies. Their tiny black round eyes stared endlessly at me.

Once I saw a speckled mare. "Greta!" I cried out, and ran to her. But all she did was slobber over my head, and I knew it could not be Greta.

I heard children singing, a familiar voice calling, "Old Man Goose! One! Two! Three!"

I ran. "Doctor Korczak!" He staggered and laughed as I crashed into him. "Doctor Korczak, are you going to the ghetto too?"

"Yes," he said, "we're all going."

"Is it wonderful?" I asked him.

He smiled. "We will make it wonderful."

I marched with the orphans. They were singing. I did not

71

know the words, so I just belted out sounds. When I was with them, I wanted to be an orphan too. Between songs came the clack and rattle of the carts and walking people. Once a voice came down from a high window: "Orphan pie!"

And then I saw Janina. She was trudging along with her family. The sack over her shoulder almost fell to the ground. I ran to her. "Janina!"

She looked at me. She smiled. "Misha!"

I burst: "Are you going to the ghetto? Where did you go? There's somebody else in your house now. I don't like him. He poured beer on my head. I smashed his foot." She laughed. I said it again. "I smashed his foot!" She laughed louder.

"Janina," I said, "nobody sees me, except Doctor Korczak."

A voice came. "They see you." It came from the man walking behind us. The piled-high cart he pulled was strapped to his shoulders. His was one of the faces I had seen around the birthday table.

"That's my father," said Janina.

"They don't look at me," I said to Janina's father. The cart behind him creaked and rattled.

"They're afraid of you," he said.

I laughed. "Nobody's afraid of me."

Janina glared at me. "Don't laugh at my father. If he says they're afraid of you, they're afraid of you."

I looked up at him. Like everyone else, he stared straight ahead. His eyes were large and chestnut brown, like Janina's.

"Why are they afraid of me?" I said.

Before he could answer, Janina piped, "Because you're not a Jew, why do you think?"

I could not imagine such a thing: people afraid of me. I took out the sausage. "Want a bite?"

"No!" came a woman's voice, but it was too late. Janina had snatched the sausage and ripped off a big bite. She handed it to her father. He looked at it for a while and finally took a bite. He held it out for the lady, but she shook her head. Another hand reached over and snatched it. This man finished it off.

"That's my uncle Shepsel," said Janina. "He lives with us."

I reached for Janina's sack. "I want to carry it."

She gave it to me and at once went skipping ahead. I slung the sack over my shoulder. It wanted to pull me backward. "What's in there?" I called.

Janina came skipping back. "All my favorite things. Except my scooter. Mama wouldn't let me bring my scooter." She glared at the lady.

I pointed to her armband. "Do you like it?" I said.

"Tobiasz—" said Janina's mother.

"Never mind," said her father. "He's the boy."

"I know. The thief."

"Never mind."

And then there was noise up ahead. The rattle of cart wheels grew louder. "Come . . . come . . ." Janina's father grunted and leaned into his harness until he was practically level to the street. The parade was going faster. Dropped pots rang like sick trolley bells. People were shouting. People were running.

16

"A closet?" said Uri.

"A closet," I said. I footed a line in the dirt, dividing our stall in half. "This big. That's what Uncle Shepsel said. 'We're living in a closet.'"

I was telling him about the day. I told him how I met Janina and her family and that everyone rushed into the ghetto, and that was how I knew the ghetto must be a wonderful place. I told him how we went into a courtyard, a dirt square surrounded by high flat walls of houses, and how Janina's father sent Uncle Shepsel—"Hurry! Hurry!"—and Uncle Shepsel dashed into one of the houses and up the stairs and Janina and I followed him but I was last because of the sack, and Uncle Shepsel planted himself in a doorway on the fourth floor and we planted ourselves too until Janina's mother and father lumbered up. And we went back down and unloaded the cart and carried the things upstairs, and some things needed two or three people to carry, but there was always one person left behind planted in the doorway, and the house was "a madhouse"—that's what Janina's mother said, "a madhouse"—because so many other people were doing the same thing and there was only one stairway and someone was planted in every doorway.

When everything was carried up, Janina's father and Uncle Shepsel broke apart the cart with hammers and kicks and carried the gray, splintery cart pieces up too, even the wheels.

When everything was finally in and Janina's father shut the door, that was when Uncle Shepsel said it: "We're living in a closet."

I told Uri what happened when I left. Janina wanted to walk down to the courtyard with me, but her mother said no. So she went with me to the landing outside the door, and then she said, "Wait" and went back inside. When she came out, she was grinning. "Close your eyes and hold out your hand." I did as she said. I felt something in my hand. "Open."

It was a piece of candy, a buttercream with a hazelnut heart. Except it was only half a candy; even half the hazelnut was gone.

"I didn't know what it was until I bit it," she said. "Then I saved it for you."

I ate it. I hadn't had one in a long time. I had thought I would never taste another. She kept grinning. I ran down the stairs.

When I returned to the ghetto, there was a wall in the way. Men were building it with bricks. It was three of me high. I walked along until I came to a section that had not yet been completed, where the wall was only a couple of bricks high. I stepped over. Someone yelled. I ran.

Running wasn't easy because again I was carrying a large sack. This time the sack was filled with food. The harvest was in and the pickings were good for quick hands and feet.

I found the house. It was on Niska Street. I climbed the stairs to the door. I knocked. A gruff voice said, "Who's there?"

"Misha Pilsudski."

I heard a squeal, then the rattle of locks. The door flew open. Janina threw up her hands. "Misha!"

Janina's mother lay on a mattress in a corner of the room. She opened one eye and grunted, "You again."

"What's that?" said Janina, pointing to the sack.

Uncle Shepsel slammed the door shut and locked it.

"Food," I said. There was a square table in the middle of the room. I dumped out the sack.

Janina clapped. "Food!"

Turnips and apples rolled onto the table and off to the floor. There were bunches of carrots and celery and loaves of bread and jars of jam and molasses and bags of sugar and links of sausage. Everyone gathered around. Even Janina's mother got up from the mattress.

"Where did you get it?" said Janina's father.

"Many places," I said.

Uncle Shepsel snapped a carrot in half. "The smelly nimble-footed thief."

Janina's mother opened up a white, dusty bag. She dipped in a fingertip, tasted it. "This is baking powder. You need an oven to bake. Does he see an oven in here?" She returned to the mattress. She lay facing the wall. "I remember ovens. I had one"—she coughed—"once. I was a human being once."

Uncle Shepsel looked at her with sad eyes. "Once upon a time."

"There's a wall outside," I said. "Why is there a wall?"

"Keep out the riffraff," said Uncle Shepsel with a sneer.

"How did you get in?" Janina asked me.

I told her how I found a low place in the wall and simply

stepped over. I added: "I can go anywhere." I was not boasting, I was simply stating a fact. I had come to love my small size, my speed, my slipperiness. Sometimes I thought of myself as a bug or a tiny rodent, slipping into places that the eye could not even see.

There was a knock on the door. Uncle Shepsel's finger flew to his lips. "Don't speak," he whispered. "We're not here." Then he sagged as Janina's father called out, "Who's there?"

"Hiram Lefkowitz," came the answer.

Janina's father unlocked the door. "Yes, come in."

As Uncle Shepsel threw a coat over the food on the table, Hiram Lefkowitz came in. He took off his hat and held out a piece of paper. "Doctor Milgrom—"

Janina's father took the paper. "I'm not a doctor." He went to a waist-high, box-looking thing squatting on the floor and pulled at it. It opened up like wings. It was a chest with many little drawers. On either side of the chest were shelves of jars, some with powders, some with liquids of different colors. It reminded me of the barbershop. I wondered how the bottles had survived the rickety trek across the city.

Janina's father took something from a drawer, put it into a little envelope, and gave it to the man. The man pulled an apple from his pocket. He looked about to cry. "I wish—"

"Go," said Janina's father, ushering the man out. "No need. Go."

The man reached back to touch Mr. Milgrom. "Shalom."

"Shalom."

Uncle Shepsel shut and bolted the door. He wagged a finger in the face of Janina's father. "By tomorrow the whole place will know. We'll be overrun."

77

Mr. Milgrom pulled in the wings, and the chest of drawers became a plain-looking box again. "What would you like me to do? Save it all for ourselves? He gave me a prescription. I did my job."

"There'll be nothing left in a week. They'll clean you out."

"Maybe we'll be out of here in a week."

"If we're out of here, it will be in our graves." He pointed out the one window. "You think they're putting up that wall only to last a week? We'll be lucky to *ever* get out of here!" He was shouting.

Janina's mother groaned on the mattress.

Janina and I were in a corner that would become our corner. "My father is a pharmacist," she told me.

"What's pharmacist?" I said.

"A pharmacist makes medicine."

"What's medicine?"

She looked at me strangely. "Medicine makes people better when they're sick. It's like pills and castor oil." She made a face. "Ugh."

"Your father is Tobiasz Milgrom," I said.

She beamed. "Yes."

"You are Janina Milgrom."

"Yes!"

"I am Misha Pilsudski!"

She clapped her hands. "Yes!"

Uncle Shepsel glared at us. Janina stuck out her tongue at him. I giggled. Not only did I have my very own last name but now I knew someone else's. I giggled as if I were being tickled.

17

Suddenly everybody was living with Uri and me in the stable. Enos the grim-faced. Kuba the clown. Ferdi the smoke blower. One-armed Olek. Shoeless Big Henryk. Gray, unspeaking Jon. And others, boys no one seemed to know.

"We stick out like purple turds," said Enos. He said that since the rest of the Jews went to the ghetto, the boys could no longer blend in with the street crowds. "And there's finches everywhere."

"What's finches?" I said.

"People that tell the Jackboots where Jews are hiding."

"I'm glad I'm not a Jew," I said.

He gave an ugly laugh. "Don't worry, the ghetto is for you too. I hear they take Gypsies. And cripples. And crazies. If you want to be safe, be a cockroach."

There must have been a finch around, because one morning as we were sleeping in the hayloft, the door flew open and voices shouted. We scrambled—like cockroaches—but Jackboots were everywhere. One of the new boys jumped from the loft. He was shot in midair and flopped to the ground floor like a rag doll.

They marched us to the ghetto. Since they had finished the brick wall—topped with broken glass and coils of barbed wire—I had not been able to visit Janina. I took this as a personal insult and challenge. I had never before been kept out of any place I wished to be, and I had no doubt that I would soon find my way to the other side of the wall. Still, I wasn't too proud to be grateful that the escorts were making it so easy.

Something else occupied my mind even more along the march: Uri. He wasn't with us. When the Jackboots rousted us in the stable, he wasn't there. This was not surprising. In recent weeks, Uri was often gone, sometimes for days at a time. With his red hair and I-belong-here invisibility, Uri believed he would never be seen as a Jew. He was fearless on the streets. Also, he believed he was much smarter than the Jackboots.

I always knew when Uri was about to disappear: he would put his fist under my chin and whisper between clenched teeth, "Don't let me hear . . ." He meant that he had appointed some of the boys to finch on me if I did something especially stupid and silly. I think he would have been surprised to know that I actually heeded his warning, as much as I was capable of heeding a warning. For some reason, I felt freer to be stupid and silly when he was there than when he was not.

It never occurred to me to worry about Uri. I believed he knew everything and could handle anything. But, prodded along by the Jackboots' rifles, I did wonder about him. Where was he? What was he doing? What would he think when he returned to find the stable empty? I did not wonder if he would find us. I knew he would.

Instead of the sidewalk, the Jackboots marched us down the middle of the streets. Horse wagons and automobiles made way for us. People stared. *We're a parade!* I thought. But for this parade the people were not silent.

"Bye-bye, you little snots!"

"Over the wall with you!"

"Filthy Jews!"

I didn't bother to tell them I wasn't a Jew.

On one street we marched down the trolley tracks, and here came a trolley heading right for us. We hesitated. The Jackboots shouted. We continued. We did not stop. The trolley did. Then, with a clank and a clang, it began to move backward, and that was how we went down the street, the trolley backing up before us as we marched on.

Soon we turned onto another street, and there was the wall. To the left and right, it went on forever in both directions. The bricks were red, the sky was brilliant blue, the knots in the barbed wire sparkled like ladies' earrings. A yellow bird landed on a curlicue of wire, stayed for a moment, and flew off.

We came to a gate in the wall. The guard opened it. We marched through. The Jackboots stayed behind. One of them bowed deeply. I didn't understand that he was mocking us. I bowed back. He kicked me in the rear end and sent me sprawling to the ground. The gate slammed shut.

I made a beeline for the Milgroms' apartment. When Janina opened the door, I announced, "I live in the ghetto now!"

"Just what we need," said Uncle Shepsel, "another neighbor."

I didn't see Janina's mother and father. "Where are your parents?"

Janina told me that her father had been taken out of the ghetto and out of the city on a work detail. Her mother was sewing uniforms for Jackboot soldiers in a Warsaw factory. Only people with work permits were allowed through the gates in the wall.

"Let's go outside!" I said.

We bolted from the apartment and ran down the stairs, Uncle Shepsel shouting, "Wear your armband!"

It was cold and bright outside. We ran about the courtyard like let-loose puppies. Uncle Shepsel's voice came down from the window. "Your armband!"

We ran out to the street. "Why don't you wear your armband?" I said to Janina.

"Why don't you?" she said.

"I'm not a Jew."

"Well, I'm just a little girl. Who cares about a little girl?" She twirled about. "Besides, we live in the ghetto now. We're safe."

We ran down the street.

To my eyes, this side of the wall looked very much like the other side: crowds of noisy people. Even the fox furs riding the shoulders of the rich ladies seemed as if they might speak at any moment.

Everywhere we went people were selling things, calling out:

"Mirror! Mirror! Unbroken!"

"Beautiful pictures! Three for the price of one!"

"Toys! Toys!"

"Hairbrush! Cheap!"

I saw a boy with one arm. "Olek!" I cried out. We ran to him. Olek squinted at us, shading his eyes with his one hand. "Olek has one arm," I said to Janina.

She punched me. "I can see." She turned to Olek. "What happened to your arm?"

Olek looked down at his right shoulder. For a moment he

seemed surprised to find the arm was gone. He frowned. "Train," he said at last.

Janina reached out. "Don't be sad. This one is good."

"This is Janina Milgrom," I announced proudly. "She's my sister."

It just came out.

Olek looked at her, but he did not smile. We all looked at each other for a while, then went our separate ways.

Later we saw gray, unspeaking Jon. He was sitting on the sidewalk, his back against the ripped wall of a bombed-out building. "Hello, Jon," I said.

Jon did not seem to hear me. His eyes were closed.

"He's sleeping," Janina whispered.

Just then one of Jon's eyes fluttered open. "This is Janina Milgrom," I said.

Janina held out her hand. "Hello."

The eye closed.

I whispered in her ear. "He doesn't talk."

Janina pulled me away. "Let him sleep," she said.

I raised my voice as if he were far away. "She's my sister."

As we walked away, I said, "Jon is gray. He's sick."

Janina said, "Why do you tell them I'm your sister? I'm not your sister."

I shrugged. I didn't know.

Before we got back to Niska Street, we heard squeals and shouts down an alley. A knot of children was writhing on the ground. Suddenly one of them, a boy, popped out of the knot and came running toward us. As he sped by, I could see that he clutched a potato in his hand. Some of the other children raced after him. The rest dragged themselves off down the alley.

Janina looked at me. "What happened?"

"Unlucky orphans," I said. I told her that was what Enos called them—orphans who did not live in Doctor Korczak's home, or any other, and who roamed the streets hungry and begging and sick.

"Be glad we're not unlucky orphans," I told her.

"Is gray Jon an unlucky orphan?" she said.

"Oh no," I said. "He's a lucky one. He's with us."

18

WINTER

Uri had found us by our first morning inside the wall. But now we saw even less of him.

"Do you go to the other side?" I asked him. "Do you have a work permit?"

"Don't ask," he said.

One cold day Uri and I were on the street. I was wearing two coats, but I could not make my feet warm. There were many people. I saw a boy. At least I thought it was a boy, from his size. He was lying on the sidewalk. I wondered how he could sleep with all the noise and people.

It was very strange. He was not in a doorway, where I had often seen people sleeping. He was not even on the edge of the sidewalk. He was right in the middle. The people just walked around him, making the shape of an eye. It was also strange that although no one seemed to see him, no one tripped over him.

But the strangest thing of all was the newspaper. It covered him like a blanket.

"Uri," I said, "that boy is stupid. The newspaper can't keep him warm."

"Nothing can keep him warm," said Uri. "He's dead."

We were stopped, looking down at the dead boy, the only ones not walking by.

"Why is he dead?" I said. "Did a Jackboot shoot him?"

Uri shrugged. "Maybe. Or no food. Or the cold. Or typhus. Take your pick."

"What's typhus?"

"A sickness. Very popular."

"Unlucky orphan."

"Yeah."

He pulled me along.

From then on, I saw dead people under newspapers every day. It was easy to tell the children—only one page was needed to cover them.

One day I asked Uri, "Why are they covered with newspaper?"

"So nobody can see them."

"But I can see them," I said.

Uri did not answer.

Then I saw one of them become seen. By a man. He stopped in front of one. He put his foot on top of the humped newspaper and tied his shoe.

The same bodies were never there two days in a row, but there were always new bodies in new places. Sometimes the feet were sticking out from the newspaper. In the first days the feet always had shoes. Then they stopped having shoes. Then the socks were gone.

In the nights I wondered who put the newspapers over the bodies, and who took the bodies away.

I thought: *Angels.*

19

The boys and I, we slept in the rubble. We did not have a blanket, but we did have a round braided rug. We all slept together under it. But that wasn't our main blanket. Our main blanket was ourselves. We slept with our arms around each other, our noses pressed into each other's necks. Enos called it trading lice. If anybody farted, he was kicked outside the rug. When Uri was with us, I slept next to him. Many nights he wasn't there. I wondered where he was, but he had said don't ask, so I didn't ask.

We were huddled kittens, the bunch of us. We were voices in the dark. Often we talked about mothers. Though I could not remember mine, I had a pretty good idea what a mother was. Not Ferdi. He was always saying, "I don't believe in them."

"Where do you think you came from?" said Enos one night under the rug. "An elephant?"

"Who do you think are all those ladies holding children's hands?" said Olek.

"Fakes," said Ferdi, whose answers were never long. He blew more smoke than words.

"Everybody has a mother," said Kuba. "Everybody."

"Orphans," said Ferdi. Whenever he spoke, you could smell his cigar breath.

"Orphans had mothers too, dummy," said Enos. "They're dead, that's all."

"Real mothers don't die," said Ferdi.

No one had an answer to that. So we talked about oranges. Like mothers, oranges were a common topic. Enos said he had eaten them many times, but Ferdi said they were only made up.

"What do oranges taste like?" I asked Enos.

He closed his eyes. "Like nothing else."

"What do they look like?"

"Like a little sun before it sets."

Ferdi said, "Oranges don't exist."

In the morning light, most of us would begin to believe in mothers and oranges again, but for now, under the rug in the pitch-blackness, hearing the faint sounds of the city from the other side of the wall, Ferdi had given us doubts.

Each morning we crawled up out of the rubble and onto the streets. Sometimes we stayed together, but mostly we went our own ways. In a group we were more of a target for the Flops, who were the ghetto police. We had no armbands, no identification papers, no records, nothing.

"We don't exist," said Ferdi under the rug one night.

Enos's voice came: "Tell that to my stomach."

Enos wasn't the only one. All of us were hungry. This was something new. Until now we had simply taken what we needed to eat. All of Warsaw had been our food market. Even in the ghetto at first, there had been food for the taking for quick hands and feet. But now, after months of winter, we were finding our hands and our stomachs empty.

Ladies no longer walked down the street with loaves in paper bags. Bakers didn't bake, as there was no flour. There were shops here and there, but the shelves were mostly empty. Where there was a morsel of food on a shelf, there was someone standing in front of it, often with a club in his hand.

Uri came with food sometimes. A jar of molasses, a turnip. When he brought chewing gum, we chewed the sugar out of it, then swallowed it whole.

Uri said, "They're starving us."

"Why?" I said.

"To get rid of us. To kill us," said Enos.

"Why don't they just shoot us?" I said.

Enos snickered. "Save money on bullets."

In the beginning there were horses in the ghetto, but then they began to disappear. Sometimes parts of them reappeared on Gesia Street. Gesia Street became an outdoor market. It was known that if you had food to sell, that was where you went. People stood on the sidewalk in the snow. Resting on an upturned crate or school desk would be the shank of a horse or a side of dog or cat, a box of salt, a licorice stick, an onion, a potato or two.

The vendors hugged themselves against the cold and cried out:

"Fat here! Nice goose fat! Twenty zlotys!"

"Bones! Bones! Crack the bones! Lots of marrow!"

"Pigeon!"

"Squirrel!"

"Dog! Dog! Best offer!"

At first the animals appeared in the market in their feathers or fur, as naturally dead as the foxes that some of the ladies still wore about their shoulders. Then, if they had fuel for fire, the vendors began to skin and pluck and roast them. The carcasses were laid out, blackened and crusty and minus their heads, and the vendors' cries went out and the prices went up.

One day I walked along Gesia Street with Enos. The smells of the roasted animals made my mouth water. I hadn't eaten since the day before. Men with clubs stood by the displays of food. Flops walked the street. Enos himself seemed not hungry but playful. He wiggled down the street and fluttered his fingers and made his voice high and fancy like a fox fur lady's and said, "Oh yes, that's lovely, I'll have that entire goose," pointing at a bird no bigger than a sparrow. "And that fine squirrel, half a pound of that, please . . . and that nostril of horse." I was laughing at Enos, and the men with the clubs were swatting at us, telling us to move on, and then I looked at Enos's face and suddenly I knew he wasn't playing after all. He winked at me. I grabbed two sparrow-size birds from under a falling club, and the both of us ran till we couldn't hear the screams behind us.

In time there were no more birds and dogs along the Gesia Street market, but the vendors never seemed to run out of squirrel. Soon everybody knew why. The charred, headless, tailless bodies laid out on the crates were not squirrels at all— they were rats—but the cry of the vendors never changed: "Squirrel! Squirrel!"

One day on my own I snatched two roasted rats. I ate one myself and took the other to Janina's house. I kept the rat in my pocket so no one would take it from me. Only Janina and Uncle Shepsel were home. Mr. Milgrom was off at the work camp, as usual. Mrs. Milgrom was at her job at the Jackboot uniform factory.

I took the rat from my pocket and held it by one leg for them to see. "I brought you a squirrel," I said.

Uncle Shepsel laughed. "Not only do you smell, you're stupid," he said between laughs. "That"—he flicked it and it swung from its leg between my fingers—"is a rat."

Janina took it from me. She made a face at Uncle Shepsel. "It's a *squirrel*. I'll save it for Mama and Tata."

Uncle Shepsel coughed. He looked around for somewhere to spit, then spit on the floor.

Janina punched his arm. "Tata said don't do that. Spit out the window."

Uncle Shepsel said, "Your mother and father know a rat when they see one. They won't eat it."

Janina stomped her foot. "It's a squirrel. They *will*. They're *hungry*."

"So am I," said Uncle Shepsel, and snatched the rat from her hand. Janina grabbed for it, and now they both had it, Janina pulling on the tiny front legs, Uncle Shepsel on the back. They grunted and scowled at each other. The rat came apart in the middle. Janina staggered backward onto her rear end. By the time she got up, Uncle Shepsel was munching on his half. She tried to reach it, but he was too tall. He kept swatting her away with his free hand as he finished off his meal.

I was there when Janina's mother came back from her job. I saw the delight on her face when Janina said, "Mama, food!" And I saw the look change when she saw what it was.

When Mr. Milgrom came in, he looked at the little half carcass and shook his head sadly and said, "No . . . not yet." He went to the mattress and lay down with Mrs. Milgrom. Janina started to cry. She threw the rat on the floor and kicked it at Uncle Shepsel. Uncle Shepsel picked it up. I left then as he was brushing floor dirt from the rat.

The next day I began walking along the wall. Until then I had not thought much about the other side. Now I thought: *There's food over there. More than rats.* The gates in the wall were guarded by Jackboots and Flops.

The wall was much too high to climb over, and even if I could get to the top, there was the thicket of barbed wire and broken glass. All that day I walked and looked, walked and looked. At last I saw something. It was not far from the uniform factory. There was a break in the bricks. It was low enough for me to reach. It was two bricks wide. I didn't know it then, but it was a drain hole of some sort. It would never occur to them that anyone could squeeze through a space two bricks wide.

I left then and came back after dark. I was through the hole in a second. I stood on the other side.

20

I expected to come back with so much food I'd have to push it one item at a time through the two-brick hole. But all I could find was a jar of fish chunks. As I squeezed back through the hole, the jar fell and broke. I picked up the chunks, brushed off the dirt, ate one, and stuffed the rest into my pockets. I went straight to the Milgroms'.

Uncle Shepsel gave his usual greeting: "Ah, the smelly one."

It was dark outside, but there was electricity this night. A single lightbulb dangled from a cord in the ceiling. Mrs. Milgrom was on the mattress. Mr. Milgrom was at the one table, seated in the only chair, doing things with his pills and bottles. There was a large purple welt on the side of his neck. It looked like an eggplant.

Janina was laughing.

"What's funny?" I said.

"You." She pointed. "You peed yourself."

I looked down. The front of my pants was soaked. It was the juice from the fish chunks in my pockets. "I have food!" I announced proudly. I pulled the fish chunks from my pockets and put them on the table. Uncle Shepsel picked one up. He sniffed it. "Pickled herring." I saw Mrs. Milgrom's head rise from the mattress.

Uncle Shepsel devoured his piece at once. Mr. Milgrom and Janina each grabbed a piece and took it over to Mrs. Milgrom. They laughed, seeing they were both doing the same thing.

Mr. Milgrom pulled Janina's head into his chest. "I'll see to Mother," he said.

Janina held her fish chunk up to the lightbulb. The skin on one side was silvery. She turned the chunk over and over, studying it. Then she licked it as if it were a taffy, each side of it. Finally, she bit off a little piece with her front teeth. As she chewed, she closed her eyes and smiled dreamily. It took her a long time to finish it.

There were only chewing sounds as they ate their chunks of pickled herring. Everyone wore coats and hats and scarves, but all had taken off their gloves, the better to feel the fish. Their frozen breaths clouded the waxy smear of light.

When the last chunk was gone, Janina pointed at me. She looked angry. "You didn't eat."

I was starting to explain that I had had a chunk before I arrived when the sound of a machine gun peppered the night. It was very near. Then there were screams and thuds and running feet and shouts: "Out! Out!"

Uncle Shepsel stood in the middle of the room and raised his hands and shouted to the ceiling, "This is it! It's over! This is it!"

"Shut up," said Mr. Milgrom as he helped his wife up from the mattress. Janina gaped at the door. It was bedlam on the other side.

"Open the door," said Mr. Milgrom calmly, "before they come in for us."

Uncle Shepsel continued to scream at the ceiling, "This is it! This is it!"

I was about to open the door when Mr. Milgrom said, "No,

wait." Slumped against one wall was a large, stuffed cloth bag embroidered in black and green designs. Mr. Milgrom reached into the bag and pulled out a blue-and-white armband. He slipped it over my coat sleeve onto my right arm. "I got this for you," he said.

I opened the door. People were stampeding by, tumbling down the stairs. Screams. Shattering glass. Gunshots.

We made our way down to the ground floor. Janina squeezed my hand. I could feel her trembling. Bright lights flooded the courtyard. I shielded my eyes. Janina nudged closer to me. Voices shrieked out of the blinding lights: "Move! Move! All you filthy sons of Abraham! All you stinking Zionists! All you dirty Jewish pigs! Line up! Line up!"

Lines were forming, like a company of soldiers. I thought: *Maybe we're going to be in a parade.* We found places. We stood.

"Silence! Silence! You filthy swine!"

Mr. Milgrom whispered, "Stand straight. Look healthy."

I heard Mrs. Milgrom groan.

As we were lining up, snow began to fall. The flakes were fat and starry in the blinding lights. "Stand at attention," Mr. Milgrom whispered. I didn't pay him much mind. He had no way of knowing how impossible it was for me to stand still. I had never stood still for more than five seconds in my life. Nevertheless, I tried. Mr. Milgrom was on one side of me, Janina on the other. The soldiers screamed. With my new armband, I thought: *I am a Jew now. A filthy son of Abraham. They're screaming at me. I am somebody.* I tried to listen well, to hear what they were screaming, but I could not understand much beyond "dirty" and "filthy" and "Jew."

Something happened up front. The screams got even louder, screechier. I heard a hollow thudding—*thock!*—as if someone were knocking wood. I leaned to the side, trying to see past the column of people in front of me. Mr. Milgrom jerked me back. "Attention!" I was beginning to get the message: Standing at attention was very important. Perhaps someone up front wasn't doing it right. I accepted the challenge. *You want attention, I'll give you attention.* I had seen many Jackboots stand at attention. I straightened my spine, snapped my heels together, lifted my chin, stared at the back in front of me. I gave them the best attention there ever was. As the screaming went on, I assumed that others were not so good at this as I.

The back I stared at was green. A lady with a green coat. Snow kept falling. Sometimes a flake tickled my nose. I did not twitch. I did not move my eyes. I barely breathed. Flake by flake the green shoulders of the lady turned white.

Somewhere up front a baby began to scream. Then another to the right. Then another. The louder the babies screamed, the brighter the lights.

"Jew dogs!"

"Filthy swine!"

Thock! Thock!

Jackboots and Flops came through the lines, screaming into the people's faces, poking them with clubs and rifles, spitting in their faces. A Jackboot stopped in front of Mrs. Milgrom. I could see from the corner of my eye. He screamed at her. She fell to the ground. "Get up, Jew dog! Filthy sow! Get up!" he screamed. *If he wants her to get up,* I thought, *why is he kicking and clubbing her?* I didn't understand. At last Mr. Milgrom managed to pull her to her feet.

The Jackboot passed by me and Janina. I think he looked at me, but I could not see his face for the blinding lights behind him. For an instant I felt proud, as if he had pinned a medal on me for standing at attention so well.

When he came to Uncle Shepsel, he growled, "Open your mouth." I heard Uncle Shepsel give a whimpering "Ohhh." He must have opened his mouth, for I saw the muzzle of a rifle come forward. I couldn't stand it any longer. I turned my head to see. I saw the muzzle go into Uncle Shepsel's mouth and push. Uncle Shepsel went backward into the lady behind him, who in turn fell back into the man behind her and so forth as the whole column of people toppled over. The Jackboot laughed.

I went back to attention. I didn't want that to happen to me.

I had known from the start that the green-coated lady in front of me was in trouble. Her attention was very poor. She wavered from side to side, sometimes her head drooped, and her shoulders were not straight at all. When a Jackboot came to her, he must have seen it also. Down came a club. *Thock!* Then another bash across her chest. The snow went flying from her shoulders into my face. I hoped the Jackboot noticed that I didn't move.

It wasn't long before the lady's shoulders were white again. Her head was drooping all the time now. I could hear her sniveling. The next time a Jackboot came to her, he said, "You stinking sow! You smell like a pig farm!" He clubbed her again, and again the snow flew from her shoulders. Then it seemed all the Jackboots were telling the people how bad they smelled. They were holding their noses. I was shocked. I had thought I was the only one who smelled bad.

I sniffed, and I began to smell it myself. I was aware of tiny yips and whimpers erupting around me. I knew what the smell was, but despite what the Jackboots said, there were really no pigs, and therefore no pig flop, in the courtyard. And then I felt down under my stomach the urge to go, and I understood what was happening. We had been standing there for a very long time, and people were having to go, and there was no place to go but where we were standing. And so people just relieved themselves where they were, and I heard the sad shudders as it ran down their legs and into the snow, and when I couldn't hold my own any longer I did the same. And even then I remained at such splendid attention I was tempted to call out to the Jackboots, *Hey, look at me!*

The screaming never stopped. By now people were falling all over the courtyard, falling and staggering to their feet and falling again. It was easy to tell the people who had not fallen: they were the ones with the highest piles of snow on their shoulders and heads. I could now feel the faint weight of the snow on my head. I wondered how it looked. I took even more pains not to move. I didn't want my snow to fall off.

I thought of the stone angel. I pictured the snow falling over it, two crests of snow rising on the tops of its wings. So silent, the both of them, the angel and the snow. I pretended I was the stone angel. I closed my eyes and pretended as hard as I could, and after a while I was convinced I could feel wings sprouting from my shoulders. I wanted to look, to see my wings, but I was an angel of stone, so I could not move.

Next thing I knew my face was in the snow and Mr. Milgrom and Janina were hauling me to my feet. "What happened?" I said.

Mr. Milgrom smacked me. "Quiet. They'll beat you. You fainted. You're too stiff. Bend your knees a little bit."

This was all getting complicated, not to mention very tiring. I was supposed to move but not move. I tried. I bent my knees. Jackboots screamed. Babies screamed. Lights screamed. We stood so long my pants dried out.

When they finally let us go, the sky was turning gray above the rooftops. We lurched across the snow. Mobs stampeded for the bathrooms. There was one on each floor. I myself did not understand bathrooms. I had never used one, never needed one. The world was my bathroom.

I dragged myself up the stairs with the Milgroms. Uncle Shepsel and Mrs. Milgrom performed a groaning duet that grew louder with each step. I followed them into the room. I wanted only to sleep. I collapsed onto the floor.

When I awoke, I thought I was back in the courtyard under the blinding lights, but it was only the sun in the window. And Uncle Shepsel, propped on his elbow, was pointing at me and saying, "Why is he sleeping here? He smells."

"I regret to inform you," said Mr. Milgrom, "that you are not a rose garden yourself these days."

Uncle Shepsel pounded the floor. "He's not family."

Mr. Milgrom looked straight at him. "He is now."

21

Kuba lifted the newspaper. "He's dead."

"Kaput," said Enos.

We were standing in the snow around the body of Jon. I wasn't sure how they could tell. Jon was no grayer, no more silent than usual. Other people walked by, not looking.

"Shoes," said Ferdi.

Jon had fine shoes, like the rest of us, except Big Henryk. When one pair wore out, we stole another.

"Somebody will take them," said Enos.

"But it's *Jon*," said Olek. He meant to point at Jon, but only his shoulder moved forward. Sometimes Olek forgot his right arm was gone.

"Give them to Big Henryk."

Uri's voice. He hadn't been there a moment ago.

"Big Henryk doesn't like shoes," I said.

This was true. Even before the ghetto, even before the Jackboots came, Big Henryk wore gray bank coin bags on his feet. Even in the snow. They were tied at his ankles with drawstrings.

"They won't fit," said Ferdi. I couldn't tell if Ferdi's cloud-breath was from the cold or his cigar.

"Big Henryk has little feet," said Uri. "Take them off."

Kuba pulled off Jon's shoes.

Uri swiped away snow with his foot. He made Big Henryk sit on the curb. He pulled off Big Henryk's bank bags. He put Jon's shoes on Big Henryk and tied them tight. Big Henryk stomped his feet like a baby. He let out a loud squawk. Uri grabbed Big Henryk's ears and twisted. I thought he was going to twist them off. Big Henryk's eyes bugged out. Using the ears as handles, Uri hauled Big Henryk to his feet. He let Big Henryk squawk some more, then said to him, "Are you going to wear the shoes?" Big Henryk nodded sharply. Uri let go.

As we were walking away, I said to Uri, "Will an angel come for Jon?" This was what I had heard under the braided rug, that when you die an angel carries you off to a place called Heaven.

Enos, overhearing, sneered. "Yeah, here comes the angel."

It was a horse, so skinny it seemed made of sticks and paper bags, clopping through the snow and slush of the street. It was led by two bedraggled men, and it pulled a wagon with a dead and naked body on it. We looked back. The horse stopped at Jon. One of the men grabbed Jon by his feet and pulled him to the wagon. The other man grabbed Jon by his armpits, and together they swung him back and forth. It reminded me of the girl orphans jumping rope. Suddenly they let go of Jon and he sailed through the air to the top of the other body. The wagon rolled on.

"Where are they taking him?" I said.

"Where do you think?" said Enos. "Off to Heaven he goes."

I believed him. "What happens there?" I said.

Kuba laughed. "He becomes a Jackboot!" Others laughed loudly, even Uri.

I was confused. "But he's dead."

"Not anymore," said Ferdi.

"Nobody is dead in Heaven, right, Uri?" said Kuba.

Everyone looked at Uri. Uri said nothing.

"They pump the air back into you and you're good as new!" said Kuba. More laughter.

Enos raised his fists. "Let's hear it for Heaven!"

Everyone cheered but Uri, even Big Henryk, and then we were silent for a long time. The only sound came from Big Henryk, trying out his new shoes, clopping them like a horse into the slush and snow. When he splattered the ankles of other people, they gave us ugly looks.

Someone gave us more than that. A Flop.

Flops were all over the place. The Jackboots hired them to guard the Jews in the ghetto. The crazy thing was, the Flops were Jews too. Jews guarding Jews! It made no sense to me.

Flops were not allowed to carry guns, but each had a whistle and a wooden club as long as my arm. They wore uniforms, but they fit no better than our clothes—no high boots, no silver eagles. And of course, being Jews, they wore armbands.

So this Flop came along and began to yell, shaking his club, "Armbands! Armbands!" As always at times like that, we scattered like cockroaches. But this time one of us got caught. Big Henryk. Big Henryk was clopping away in his new shoes and did not notice anything else until the Flop had him by the arm. I heard a bellow and stopped to look back. Big Henryk was standing in front of the Flop, holding his head with both hands while the Flop screamed at him and waved the club in his face. The Flop was short and scrawny. He had to look up at Big Henryk as he screamed at him.

Then I saw a flash of red hair. It was Uri coming up behind

the Flop. He grabbed the club and pulled the Flop over backward to the sidewalk.

By now the rest of the people were on the other side of the street, pretending they didn't see. Now the club was in Uri's hand and Big Henryk was just standing there watching, and that was when Uri conked the Flop on the top of his head. Just like that: *thock!* Like the sounds in the lineup.

Now it was the Flop holding his head, wobbling about the sidewalk. This must have tickled Big Henryk, for he took the club from Uri and bopped himself in the head. That must have tickled the rest of us, for suddenly we were all dashing out of our shadows, passing the club around, bopping ourselves in the head just hard enough to be fun and send us lurching around the wobbling Flop. When the Flop lost his balance and toppled to the ground, we got other notions. We pulled off his shoes and flung them into the street, and all the people on the other side suddenly had eyes and dove for the shoes. And then the Flop's jacket went flying, and then his pants.

"Take his feet," Uri said to Enos, and Enos took his feet and Uri took his arms, and I was having too much fun to think: *Uri, you're not being invisible.* They swung him like a jump rope, like the wagon men had swung dead Jon, and let him fly, and the Flop went sailing through the air, landing in a slushy splash. Uri wound up and flung the club far into the rubble, and the Flop groaned in the snow in his underwear, and once again there were no eyes on the other side of the street.

22

SPRING

"Here comes the big shot," said grim-faced Enos.

"The new Jew," said Kuba the clown.

"The family man," said Ferdi. His cigar flapped in his mouth as he spoke.

"The littlest Jew," said Enos. "We are honored by your presence." He stood and bowed to me.

Uri smiled.

I no longer slept all the time with the boys. Sometimes, over Uncle Shepsel's objections, I slept at the Milgroms'. When I returned to sleep with the boys, they ribbed me. There were mountains of rubble to climb over to reach the braided rug. We slept on top of it now. It was spring.

From the moment Mr. Milgrom said, "He is now," my identity as a Gypsy vanished. Gone were the seven wagons, seven brothers, five sisters, Greta the speckled mare. Deep down I guess I had always known my Gypsy history was merely Uri's story, not reality. I didn't miss it. When you own nothing, it's easy to let things go. I supposed my last name was Milgrom now, so Pilsudski went too. I kept Misha. I liked it.

I kept something else too—the yellow stone around my neck. The yellow stone my father had given me. I knew, as something in me had always known, that that was the one true part of Uri's story.

We lounged on the rug, on our backs, our hands behind our heads, taking it easy, enjoying the mild air, watching the stars fade. Soon there was only the moon and one star. A smear of robin's-egg blue showed beyond the rubble. Day was coming.

We were night people now. We were all smugglers now, even Big Henryk. Smuggling was a nighttime thing.

Ferdi passed around his cigar. We took turns puffing and coughing. The stars were fuzzy beyond the cigar smoke.

"Himmler coming!"

These words were followed by the silence of surprise, as they were spoken by Big Henryk, who often bellowed like a cow but hardly ever bellowed words.

At last Enos said, "Himmler? *The* Himmler?"

"Himmler coming," Big Henryk repeated.

"I don't believe it," said Enos.

"Why is he coming?" said one-armed Olek.

Enos asked Uri, "What do *you* think?"

Uri had the cigar. He blew a stream of smoke at the stars. "I think Himmler can go anywhere he wants."

"Who's Himmler?" I said.

Enos laughed.

"Just the Number Two Jackboot, that's all," said Kuba, who had taken a seat on a pile of bricks.

"You can thank Himmler for this wonderful bedroom," said Enos. "And for the growl in your stomach. And the bodies in the streets. And the wall."

"Himmler Schmimmler," said Kuba.

"We're as good as dead," said Enos.

"Himmler coming!" bellowed Big Henryk.

The sun came up and we went to sleep. We woke at noon and scattered. I looked for Himmler everywhere. I didn't see him. I was disappointed. I wanted to get a look at the Number Two Jackboot. I had heard of a man called Hitler, who was boss of all the Jackboots, who were also called Nazis. But it was Himmler, Enos said, who was in charge of the ghetto. In charge of the Jews. In charge of us.

I usually brought food to the Milgroms. This time it was news: "Himmler is coming!" I announced. After giving me his greeting—"Ah, the smelly intruder"—Uncle Shepsel looked me over and said, "Where's the food?"

Mr. Milgrom was lancing a boil on his wife's leg. "A little gratitude would be nice."

"I hate Himmler," said Janina. She was playing pick-up-sticks on the floor. She had brought them from the old house.

"Don't you want to see him?" I said.

"If I see him," she said, "I'm going to go right up and kick him." To show me, she stood and kicked the leg of the table.

"Who says he's coming?" said Uncle Shepsel.

"Big Henryk," I said.

"Who's Big Henryk?"

"He's big," I said. "He didn't used to wear shoes. Now he wears dead Jon's."

"I'll stop there," said Uncle Shepsel. "Are you going for food?"

"Not now," I said.

"I'm hungry now."

Mr. Milgrom snapped: "Shepsel!"

Uncle Shepsel slunk back into his usual corner. Mr. Milgrom finished with the boil and pulled Mrs. Milgrom up to a sitting position, her back against the wall. She had become skinny and gray. She no longer worked at the uniform factory. She tilted to one side. Her hair was like a mop. She looked like rag dolls I had seen Doctor Korczak's orphan girls carry. She coughed, and the force of the cough toppled her over. Mr. Milgrom straightened her up again.

He pushed himself to his feet. He shuffled across the room to me. I knew he was going to talk to me. He seemed to feel he had to be close to me in order to speak. And he never spoke without touching me. Sometimes he laid his hand on my head, sometimes he ran his fingertip across my shoulder. He did this with Janina too. And he always smiled when he spoke to us.

"You're a good boy," he said.

I was sure he was about to praise me more, but Janina interrupted. "Am I a good girl?" she said, pressing up to his leg.

He laid his other hand on her head. "You are both good. You are the best children."

"But who's better," said Janina, "Misha or me?"

Mr. Milgrom looked down on us. His smile seemed to double, so we would both have a full share. He pretended to give the question great thought. "No one is better," he said at last. "It's a tie."

Janina stomped her foot. "Tata! It can't be a tie. Somebody *has* to be better."

"Who says?" said her father.

"Tata! I beat Misha all the time when we race." (This was a lie. It was I who always won. Janina lied a lot.) "And I'm better at pick-up-sticks." (True.) "And look." She did a split. "And *look*." She attempted a headstand. For a few seconds her feet hung in the air inches above the floor. Her shoes were caked with spring mud, crusty and torn. The shoes came back down. She stood proudly. "See." In her mind she had done a magnificent feat. "I can do that for a whole hour if I want to."

Mr. Milgrom nodded. "Very impressive. It's still a tie."

Janina stomped. She squealed. Mr. Milgrom raised his finger. She stopped squealing. She started again when he put his finger down. He raised it again. She stopped.

"But, Tata, you said I'm wonderful. Remember you said that?"

"I remember," he said. "And I meant it."

Janina stuck out her tongue at me. "*I'm* wonderful."

"And so is he," said Mr. Milgrom.

"But I'm *more* wonderful, right, Tata?"

"You are both equally wonderful," said Mr. Milgrom. "You are each wonderful in your own way."

"What way am I wonderful, Tata?"

He sat down with a sigh in the only chair. He was always tired. He was no longer smiling, and yet it felt somehow as if he was. "You"—he pressed the tip of her nose with his finger—"are girl wonderful. And he is boy wonderful."

Janina looked at me. She was the only person I knew who had to look up at me. She studied me. She turned back to her father. "But girl wonderful is better than boy wonderful, yes, Tata?"

Mr. Milgrom slumped in the chair. He wagged his head. He turned Janina around by her shoulders and gave her a gentle pat on the backside. "Go play pick-up-sticks with Misha," he said.

We had just sat down cross-legged on the floor, the pick-up-sticks between us, when we heard voices in the courtyard. I couldn't make out what they were saying. I went to the window and leaned out. Now I could hear:

"Himmler's coming!"

23

Janina was screaming as I raced down the stairs to the courtyard and the street. She wanted to kick Himmler, and it took
both her father and Uncle Shepsel to hold her back.

I careened from person to person. "Where is Himmler? . . .
Where is Himmler?" I followed pointing fingers down one
street and another until I saw the cars coming, a parade of
them. Huge cars, magnificent cars, with the tops down. The
cars had uniforms of their own. They were gray and silver and
unsmiling and proud, like the men sitting in them. Peddlers'
carts veered out of the way. I was surprised that people were not
pouring out of the buildings, mobbing the sidewalks. A few
people stood at the curb, hats in hand, looking down. Others
kept walking along, eyes straight ahead. Such was a man whose
sleeve I tugged. "Which one is Himmler?" The man kept moving as if I wasn't there. Only the Flops looked at the parade.
They stood at attention with one arm outthrust in the Jackboot
salute, as if reaching for something no one else could see. A corner of newspaper over a nearby corpse waved in the breeze.

I began to panic. I grabbed at people. "Which one is
Himmler?" No one would answer. I trotted along with the cars.
I stared at the magnificent men. They stared straight ahead.
On their Jackboot hats the great silver eagles spread their
wings and seemed to glare at the people, daring them to do
something wrong. Their wings were like angels' wings, except
the eagles' wings were fully unfurled, flying.

I began calling to the men in the cars. "Are you Herr Himmler?"

Some of the men looked down at me. No one answered. I ran from car to car. "Are you Herr Himmler?" I saw a man, the most magnificent Jackboot I had ever seen, sitting in the back-seat of the first car. *It must be him!* His ramrod attention was better than my own in the courtyard, and he was only sitting. Blond hair curled from beneath his eagle-winged hat. His head looked as if it had been chiseled from stone. His jawbone was all the weapon he would ever need. "Herr Himmler!" I shouted. "Herr Himmler!" He did not move.

But someone else did.

The Jackboot in the passenger side of the front seat turned his head slightly, enough so that one of his eyes stared at me for a moment. The eye seemed too large, as it was magnified behind the thick, round lens of his eyeglasses. The only thing magnificent about this man was his uniform. I saw half a little black mustache—it seemed to be dripping out of his nostril—a scrawny neck, a head that seemed more dumpling than stone. *Can this be Himmler? The Number Two Jackboot?* He couldn't be. He looked like Uncle Shepsel!

I knew how to prove it one way or the other. His boots. Surely on the feet of Himmler, Master of All the Jews, would be the most magnificent boots of all. Maybe they went all the way up his legs. Maybe they had silver eagles.

The parade was picking up speed. I ran to keep up. "Herr Sir! Let me see your boots! Herr Sir!"

And suddenly I was on the ground. I had run smack into someone. As I got to my feet, a club was swinging back and forth before my eyes. I heard a loud smacking kiss. There was an overpowering smell of mint. Beyond the swinging club the parade rolled through an open gate in the wall and was gone.

I knew who was on the other end of the club. I looked up. It was Buffo. Buffo was the worst Flop of all. He was the only one I was really afraid of. We all were.

No one knew how to account for an existence like Buffo's. It did not seem that he could possibly be a Jew, but then he wasn't a Jackboot either. We boys decided to believe he was a Warsaw sausage maker—he looked like a pile of fat sausages—who hated Jews so much that he pretended to be one so that he could live in the ghetto. Then he could become a Flop and torment Jews to his heart's content.

Like all Flops, Buffo was not allowed to carry a gun, but that made no difference to him. He would not have shot anyone if he could. He carried only his club. It was said that he loved the sound of his club cracking open a skull like a pumpkin, but this was not true. He hardly ever used his club. His real weapons were his hands.

More than anything, he loved killing Jews with his hands. And not just any Jews. Jewish children. If you were an adult Jew, he would walk right past you, but he went out of his way for children. Sometimes he left the streets and waddled through the alleyways and rubble, smacking his club on his thigh, hunting. When he spotted someone to go after, he kissed the club. Fortunately, he was fat and slow. If he managed to catch you or trick you, he used the club to stun you. Then he jammed it into his belt and waggled his fingers for the treat to come.

He always smelled of mint. Not from chewing gum or candy. From mint leaves. He chewed them like some men chewed tobacco. There were always tiny flecks of mint on his lips. If you could see them, and if you could smell the mint, you knew you were too close. In fact, that was how we came to say a child was killed by Buffo: "He smelled the mint."

His favorite way to kill you was to pull you face-first into his bottomless belly and smother you. When this happened, the odor of mint hovered about the body until the wagon came to cart it away.

I think Buffo hated me most of all. I was the only one who ever got close enough to smell the mint and lived to tell of it. Though he terrified me, I pestered him. I couldn't help myself. I called him Fatman. I had no sense. If I had had sense, I would have known what all the other children knew: The best defense against Buffo was invisibility. Never let him see you.

Me? If I saw him waddling down the street, I would sneak up behind him and yell, "Fatman!" He would be fuming as he turned around, for he recognized my voice—his personal gnat—and the club would already be swinging and I would be ducking out of the way. "Your ears are hairy!" I would shout, and thumb my nose at him and scoot away into the crowd.

And now here he was, looming above me, smiling and kissing his club, and that was giving me all the time I needed to get away—but I couldn't. He had my foot pinned to the ground with his boot (a scuffed, mud-caked, un-Jacklike boot). I screamed in pain. He laughed. The club clattered to the street—he wasn't going to use it. He was going to drown me in his belly. His meaty hands gripped my shoulders. I was dizzy with mint. My nose sank into his belly. And suddenly I was loose. I had yanked myself out of the shoe he had pinned to the ground, and now I was running, bouncing off people.

When it was safe to stop, I sat on a curb. I had foiled Buffo again. I was alive. I took the other shoe off and threw it away. It was spring. When the cold came back, I would steal another pair.

That night on the rug, I laughed as I told the other boys about my close call with Buffo.

Uri did not laugh. He said, "Don't."

"Don't what?" I said.

"Don't bait Buffo."

"Why?" I said.

He smacked me, hard, three times. "Don't," he repeated. The rest of the boys were silent.

I turned away and whimpered myself to sleep. I never mentioned the man who could not have been Himmler.

24

"Find the cow," Doctor Korczak had said.

It was the only time Doctor Korczak was ever stern with me. Whenever I brought him food for the orphans from the other side of the wall, he received it happily and patted me on the head and said, "My little smuggler." And as I turned to go, he never failed to say, "Be careful." Then one day he added, "Find the cow." From then on, every time I saw him: "Find the cow."

The cow had become something to believe in or not to believe in. Like angels. Mothers. Oranges. How could something as large as a cow live in the ghetto and not be seen? How could it survive? What would it eat? Rubble dust?

And yet so great was the cry for milk for children that the cow seemed to materialize from the very hunger of the people, until one could almost see the animal loping down the street. Of course, no one really did see it, and the more we did not see it, the more we believed in it. Almost every day someone claimed to have heard a mysterious moo.

Of course, the day soon came when Janina said she heard it.

"No, you didn't," I said, just to be contrary. Janina was always making things up.

"I *did*!" she said. We were playing pick-up-sticks. She swept the sticks away.

"You're being a baby," I said.

"You're being a poop," she said.

Uncle Shepsel looked up from the book he was reading and growled at Janina. "There's no cow."

Reading the new book he had found was all Uncle Shepsel did these days. When he reached the end of the book, he went back to the first page and started again. He muttered under his breath as he read. It was a book about the Lutherans. He was teaching himself to be one. Then he would no longer be a Jew, and they would let him out of the ghetto.

Mr. Milgrom told him, "You cannot stop being a Jew."

Uncle Shepsel said, "I've already stopped. I'm a Lutheran."

When Uncle Shepsel growled at Janina that there was no cow, I switched to her side. "Yes, there is," I said. "I heard it too." Until then, I had been uncertain. From that moment on, I believed in the cow. (I had done this before: it seemed I believed whatever I heard myself say.) A few days later, when Doctor Korczak first said, "Find the cow," my belief was confirmed.

I could not find the cow. I looked all over. Courtyards, backyards, cellars, rubble. No cow. No moo.

"I can't find the cow," I complained to the boys one day.

"That's because there is no cow, stupid," said Enos.

Big Henryk bellowed, "No cow!"

Kuba climbed up Big Henryk and sat on one of his shoulders. "I'll bet Big Henryk is lying," he said. Kuba leaned down so that his face was upside down in front of Big Henryk's. "Big Henryk, do you believe there's a cow?"

Big Henryk swayed under the weight of Kuba. "Yes!" he said.

We all laughed because we knew his answer proved nothing. Big Henryk was not only the biggest boy but also the most agreeable. He said yes to everything.

116

This was our signal to play the Big Henryk game.

"Big Henryk, do you believe you're the biggest, dumbest person in the whole wide world?"

"Yes!"

"Big Henryk, do you believe you're a little itty-bitty baby?"

"Yes!"

"Big Henryk, are we going to sleep in a castle tonight in big soft beds and eat all the chocolates we want and the Jackboots will be our servants?"

"Yes!"

"Ask him if he believes in Buffo," said Enos. "Or Himmler."

"Big Henryk, do you believe in Himmler?"

I butted in. "I don't," I said. "There is no Himmler." And I told them at last about the parade of magnificent cars and how I called and called Himmler's name and the only one who turned was the chicken-looking man in the front seat, turning one eye to stare at me behind the eyeglass.

"That was Himmler," said Uri.

"He can't be," I said. "He looks like my uncle Shepsel."

"It's him," said Uri.

So Himmler—Number Two Boss Jackboot, Master of All Jews Not to Mention Gypsies—was a one-eyed chicken. At that moment, I began losing respect for Jackboots. I no longer wanted to be one.

25

SUMMER

There were no longer bows in Janina's hair or socks on her feet. The straps on her shoes were broken and flapped when she walked. The shoes had become muddy scraps. For a while I tried to shine them with spit, but the mud was too much. The best reflection I had ever seen of myself disappeared with the shine of her shoes.

Janina cried a lot. And kicked. And screamed. Sometimes she screamed at her mother. "Mama, Mama, make me a pickled egg! . . . Make me! . . . Make me!" She loved pickled eggs more than anything, she said. But her mother only lay with her back to the room on the mattress in the corner.

As much as Janina cried, she laughed too. But she didn't just laugh—she howled. Especially when I told her that Himmler looked like Uncle Shepsel. We were sitting on the floor picking each other's lice at the time, and Uncle Shepsel had just said, "You look like monkeys," and I had whispered to Janina, "Himmler looks like Uncle Shepsel," and Janina burst out laughing so hard she fell backward and knocked her head on the floor and lice flew from her hair, and the head knock really hurt and Janina didn't know whether to laugh or cry, so she did both.

* * *

One day Janina ran to me in the courtyard. "I found the cow!" she screamed, and grabbed my hand and we ran. She led me to a bombed-out ice cream shop. Two walls were still standing. On one of them hung a tilting picture—of a cow.

She often played such tricks on me. Once, she tricked me into lending her my yellow stone necklace. She wore it for days. When I asked for it back, she threw it over the wall. I couldn't believe it.

I was so mad I threw the bag of gifts she had left on the steps for me over the wall.

She threw my cap over the wall.

She had brought one toy animal with her from the other side—a blue-and-gold stuffed pig. She hid it. I found it and threw it over the wall.

She said no more. She said even though I threw away her things, she was going to give me something new. I believed her. I felt bad. She said the new gift was already under my coat-bed. I looked. It was a rat bone.

She liked to goad me into chasing her. Whether I did or not, she always ran. If I didn't chase her, she would stop and thumb her nose at me and call me "Feeshy Meeshy!" I didn't have to be goaded the time she leaned out of the window above me and dropped a raw turnip on my head. I picked the turnip out of the dirt, put it in my pocket, and took off after her. When I caught her, I shook her and told her never to treat food that way. All she did was laugh, so I rubbed the dirty turnip in her face and shook her harder, and the harder I shook, the louder she laughed.

I became so used to her noise—chattering, whining,

pestering, laughing, crying—that my ear went on hearing it even when it stopped. All during one particular day I sensed that something was wrong, but I didn't know what. I didn't know it was the absence of Janina. I barely heard her all day, barely saw her. That night, as usual, most activity came to a stop. The lightbulb was always dark now. The end of the day's light was the end of ours. No more knocks on the door for Mr. Milgrom's pills and potions. Uncle Shepsel put away his book on how to become a Lutheran. Mrs. Milgrom did not have to stop whatever she was doing, for she did nothing to begin with. All day, all night, she lay on the mattress with her back to us. She moved only when she coughed.

Usually Janina continued to play pick-up-sticks in the dark—by fingertip feel—until her father said, "Janina," and she would stop and lie down on the overcoat next to me. But on this night she was already on her coat when I lay down. I slept with my new family almost every night now. Mr. Milgrom always said good-night to us, first to Janina, then to me. I always looked forward to that moment, as no one had ever said good-night to me before. On this night, when he said, "Good night, Janina," there was no answer.

As usual, I waited until I heard everyone sleeping. It pleased me to do this. I liked to pretend that if anyone heard me go out, I would be forbidden. I got up and crept from the room. I did this nearly every night. I tiptoed down the stairs and into the moonlit courtyard and into the street. My instinct was to be bold and uncatchable, but I enjoyed being sneaky too.

The streets looked deserted, but I knew they were not as deserted as they appeared. I knew that somewhere along the wall Big Henryk stood as tall as he could with Kuba on his shoulders, and Kuba was draping two thick coats across the barbed wire and hauling himself over and down to the other side, then tossing over the wall the rope that Big Henryk would winch him back with.

I knew that beneath my feet, in the sewers where daylight never fell on the rats and the rivers of poop, Enos and Ferdi and one-armed Olek were creeping toward the wall, puffing on Ferdi's cigars to give themselves points of light and to smoke over the stink.

I knew they all wished they could come with me. They wished they could fit through the two-brick space.

As for Uri, who knew? He was somewhere, doing something.

I darted from shadow to shadow until I was across the street from the wall. I stood in the shadow of a doorway. The night glowed beyond the barbed wire. Sounds floated over: a clink, a tinkle, a voice, a wisp of music. I leaned out to watch for Flops on patrol. Someone was standing in the moonlight an arm's length away. I couldn't believe it.

"Janina!"

"I followed you."

She was grinning. I yanked her into the doorway.

"Go back," I said.

"No."

"Go *back*."

"I'm going with you."

Her eyes were two drops of moonlight.

"You're not little enough," I said stupidly.

"I'm littler than you."

"I'm not taking you."

"You have to. You're my big brother."

That stopped me for a moment. And gave me all the more reason not to allow her.

"No!"

"Yes!"

I smacked her in the face. The moon drops wobbled.

She smacked me back.

And that was that.

I dashed across the street to the wall, and in a moment I was through the two-brick space and onto the other side. A moment later she came squirting through the hole.

26

She stood gaping. "The rest of the city—it's still here!"

I ran to her. I pulled the armband from her sleeve and stuffed it into her coat pocket. I did the same with my own. "See, you made me forget." I stomped off.

It was not good to be seen near the wall. I took the sidewalks. I heard her footsteps behind me. I walked fast. Maybe I couldn't stop her from following me, but I had no intention of making her a full partner.

Soon we were among the people, the source of the voices and sounds that came drifting over the wall. In the ghetto all was gray: the people were gray, the sounds were gray, the smells were gray. Here everything was colors to me: the red clang of the streetcars, blue music from phonographs, silver laughter of people. In the distance the tootles of the merry-go-round were a swirl of colors. Whenever I came through the wall, I wanted to do nothing but walk the streets.

I remembered Uri's words: *Don't look guilty.* I swaggered down the sidewalk. I headed straight for other pedestrians and made them veer around me. I whistled. In other words, I ignored Uri's other commands: *Don't call attention to yourself. Be invisible.* Or maybe I heeded a little. I resisted the temptation to put the blue-and-white band back on my arm. I was proud to be part of the Milgrom family, proud to be a Jew. I wanted to wave my armband and shout, *Hey, everyone, look at me, I'm a Jew! A filthy son of Abraham!* But I didn't.

I heard Janina whistling behind me.

I went to my favorite place. It was a hotel for Jackboots. Jackboots ate there and drank beer and slept there. A blue neon sign in the shape of a camel blinked off and on above a revolving door. I did what I always did: I went in the revolving door and around and right back outside again. Janina did it too, but she didn't stop after once around. I jerked her away.

I went around back. Garbage cans as tall as me were lined up like soldiers. As usual, the lids were off, and several children were poking through the stench and maggots. They were too busy to notice me. The hatch door leading to the food cellar was locked, as usual. There were several windows at ground level. There were steel bars in front of the glass.

I knelt before one of the windows. I pushed it open. I took off my coat and tossed it inside. I turned myself sideways and squeezed between two of the bars and dropped headfirst into the dimly lit cellar. I thought nothing of it. I lived in the cracks of a world made for large, slow people.

As I was bending over for my coat, Janina's coat hit me in the rump. She came tumbling down in a flurry of underwear. "Ow!" she squawked.

"Be quiet," I told her. "You should have stayed home."

I pulled the sack from my pocket and unfolded it.

"What's that for?" she said.

"Food," I said.

"I don't have one."

"Too bad."

"Where's the pickled eggs?"

"They don't have any." Not that I would have known a pickled egg if I saw one.

She swept a large coffee can from a shelf. It crashed to the floor.

I balled my fist in front of her face. "Stop it. They're going to hear."

She jabbed her chin at me. "I don't like you."

"I don't like you."

"Good," she said, and stomped off among the shelves, searching for pickled eggs.

I began making my rounds. There was one problem with the blue camel hotel food cellar: much of the food was in cans and jars too big and heavy to carry a long way. So I concentrated on smaller, lighter things. There were wooden bins of onions and lettuces and turnips and cabbages. There were boxes of soda crackers and stacked loaves of brown and black bread. There were gray, ancient dried fish and jellies and potatoes sprouting wigs of grass. I avoided the cold locker of fresh meats, as we had no way to cook them, but shriveled clubs of sausage were perfect.

I filled my sack and headed for my treat. Although the jars of fruits and vegetables were too big to carry, who was to say I could not help myself to them right there in the food cellar? I pulled out from a dusty corner my personal jar of peaches in syrup. The jar was almost as big around as myself. I unscrewed the lid and grabbed a peach.

"What's that?" came Janina's voice at my shoulder.

"What's it look like?" I stuffed the peach into my mouth.

"I want one." She reached.

I smacked her hand. "They're mine."

She balled her fists, leaned back, and screamed, "I'm hun-greee!"

I grabbed another peach and stuffed it into her mouth. "Here." I quick closed the jar and shoved it back just as a door opened and light flooded from above. Footsteps came partway down the stairway and stopped. A voice said, "Hello? . . . Hello?"

We crouched by the fruit jars, our cheeks bulging, peach juice streaming from our chins.

"Hello?"

At last the footsteps went away and the door closed. I pushed a crate under the window and climbed onto it. I shoved the stuffed sack—and then myself—through the bars. Even standing on the crate, Janina could not reach, so I had to help haul her out.

Going back, I lugging the sack over my shoulder, we stayed in the shadows and alleyways until the final dash across the moonlight to the two-brick space and onto the other side. Another dash across the moonlight and back into the shadows.

I headed for the orphanage. Doctor Korczak always left a window unlocked in the back. I opened it and dumped in half the contents of my sack.

"What are you doing?" said Janina.

"Feeding the orphans," I told her.

"You're supposed to feed us."

I was tired of her crabbing. "I feed whoever I want to feed." I slammed the window shut and headed home.

27

The next day I visited the boys. I knew I would find them in their new place, an alley behind a fire-gutted butcher shop. Before I got there I could hear them: a whacking sound followed by cheers . . . and again *whack!* then cheers. What was happening? I turned the corner. Big Henryk was holding Kuba upside down by his ankles while Ferdi walloped Kuba's rump with a big bone, one of the many that were lying around.

Ferdi stopped when he saw me. "Misha! Come on. Knock out your lice."

Then I saw. Each time Ferdi walloped Kuba, a tiny blizzard, like salt, fell from Kuba's hair to the ground. With every blow Kuba swung back and forth like the pendulum of a grandfather clock. When it was over, Kuba took the bone from Ferdi. He said, "Your turn, Mish." Just because he made me think of it, my head was itching more than ever. I could feel them crawling.

I got down on all fours in front of Big Henryk. In a moment I was hanging upside down, staring at his knees. "Get ready," said Kuba, and then I heard Ferdi's voice, "Wait! The book!" Ferdi stuffed a book down my pants, and the world shook as Kuba gave me the first wallop. Another voice came screaming, "Stop it! Stop it!"

I twisted my head as best I could and saw Janina attacking Kuba, kicking him, punching him. Ferdi grabbed her, held her flailing.

"I'm not hurting him," said Kuba.

"Who is this?" said Enos.

"This is Janina," I said as Kuba swung the bone. Then between wallops: "My . . . sis . . . ter . . ."

By the time Kuba was done with me, Janina was yapping, "Me! Me!"

She was heading for Big Henryk when Enos said, "You can't have a girl in a dress hanging upside down. She needs pants."

I was the littlest, so I was elected. I took off my pants and gave them to Janina. I stuffed in the book, and upside down she went and Kuba started walloping away. With each spank she gave a yelp and a laugh.

I had a thought: *Maybe her angel will come out.* This was my latest information from the boys on angels: Every person carries his or her own angel inside. When the rest of you is killed, the angel comes out and flies off to Heaven. When I asked where Heaven is, everyone had a different answer.

Kuba said Russia.

Olek said Washington America.

Enos said, "You're all stupid. It's right here. Warsaw. The other side of the wall."

As I watched Janina's little body jump with every spank, I couldn't imagine the angel inside her putting up with such a disturbance. I stared and stared, but nothing came out of her but yelps and laughs and lice.

Kuba finally stopped. Janina was begging for more. She wouldn't give up my pants. Everyone laughed as I chased her around the rubble, the book bouncing in the pants like a load of horse flop. Suddenly the laughter stopped. I turned around.

Four people were standing at the corner of the charred butcher shop. Everyone, even Janina, stopped and stared at them.

They were two couples. The men were Jackboots. Their buttons glinted like morning stars on their uniforms. The ladies were blond-haired and wore little white hats and white gloves. All four of them were smiling.

One of the Jackboots was holding something. It was black. I was pretty sure it was a gun or a weapon. I wondered: *Why aren't we running?* And then I saw movement—Janina was walking toward them. I called out, "Janina! No!"

Still smiling, the Jackboot raised the weapon. He held it up to his eye, aiming it at her.

"No!"

I charged into the Jackboot. He didn't budge. He reached down with his free hand and tossed me aside. He aimed again through the weapon at Janina. I heard: *click.*

Enos called, "Misha, stop. It's a camera. It takes pictures."

I didn't know what he was talking about, but I backed off. The man with the camera aimed and clicked again. Beside me, Janina was doing a dance in the dust and smiling at the camera man and saying, "Do it again! . . . Again!"

The couples were no longer just smiling, they were laughing out loud. The ladies were clinging to their men's arms to keep from falling over with laughter. Then one of the ladies pinched her nose, and the other pinched her nose, and they laughed louder and the camera man took more pictures. And the more they laughed and took pictures, the faster Janina danced and laughed. The dust she kicked up fell on their shoes.

When the laughing died down, Janina stepped forward. She

walked up to one of the ladies and said, "Do you live on the other side?" The lady did not answer. She just looked down and smiled. Then Janina reached out and touched the skirt of the lady's black-and-white checkerboard dress. The lady's smile vanished. She stepped back from Janina's reach. She looked down at the dust on her white shoes. She said something to the others. The smiles came back.

The man taking pictures gave the camera to his lady. He motioned to Janina and me to stand side by side. He stood behind us. I could feel him smiling. He was close, but he never touched us. He said something to the lady. She aimed and clicked.

Maybe they'll shoot us now, I thought.

But they didn't. They merely went away. As they were leaving, I called, "Aren't you going to shoot us?"

They didn't respond. Enos hurried over. "Stupid Gypsy." He smacked the back of my head. "Learn to shut your stupid mouth."

I wished Uri were there. I preferred that he do the smacking.

"Who were they?" said Ferdi.

"Soldiers with their girlfriends," said Enos. "Out for a stroll in the ghetto. It's Sunday."

"What's Sunday?" I said.

Enos sneered. "The day they don't shoot you."

Back on the streets, we saw other soldiers and girlfriends strolling about.

The Jackboot ladies wore white gloves. I couldn't stop staring at the gloves. They were whiter than snow.

28

Summer was flies. I thought of them as little birds. I remembered real birds. I remembered them singing as I lay in tall grass that smelled like carrots. Except for crows, birds did not come to the ghetto. There was no bread for them to eat, no seed. The crows that came did not sing. They squawked at each other. They seemed to say, *Over here! I found one!* Or, *Stay away! This is mine!* There was always plenty for them to eat. They ate people. Crows and flies.

The wagons came in the morning. There had been a few horses left, pulling the morning wagons, but the Jackboots took them, so now men became horses. When the wagon came to a body, it stopped and the men went to the body. Not all bodies were dead. If a body had flies but no crow, it might still be alive, especially if it also had no newspaper over it. Sometimes crows pecked away the newspaper.

When the men came to a body, the crows usually walked away. They walked five or six steps and turned and squawked at the men. One man took hands, one took feet, and they flopped the body onto the wagon. When the body flopped onto the pile, the whole wagonload of flies jumped into the air like lice from a walloper. Then they settled back down again, and a crow or two landed and went along for the ride.

I used to think that if a body had no shoes or socks or coat, it was dead. But then I saw one such body climb out from under the pile on a wagon and walk away. The men had made a mistake. But you could count on crows. They never made a mistake.

Some people died from sickness, some from hunger. There wasn't much I could do about the sickness, but hunger, that was where I came in. Feeding my family—and as much as possible Doctor Korczak's orphans—was what the world had made me for. All the parts—the stealing, the speed, the size, the rash stupidity—came together to make me the perfect smuggler.

Janina followed me everywhere. My shadow. I went through the wall at night, and there she was, behind me, with a sack of her own. I never spoke to her. I pretended she wasn't there.

We raided the blue camel hotel. We raided the finest homes in Warsaw. We had many favorite kitchens. One was a special favorite because we always found pickled herring there. We must have felt very comfortable in that kitchen, because we always turned the light on. One night we were sampling the herring when I heard Janina say, "Hello." I turned. A little boy was standing in the doorway. He wore pajamas. He was squinting in the light.

The boy mumbled, "Who are you?"

"I am Janina," she said. She suddenly seemed very grown up. She pointed to me. "This is Misha."

The boy kneaded his fists in his eyes. "Are you Jews?"

Janina laughed. "Ha-ha! Jews? Oh no, we would never be Jews. Not us. Ha-ha!" She held out a piece of herring. "Want some fish?"

The boy took the fish, and for the next hour the three of us sat around the kitchen table eating pickled herring and crackers and sugar cookies and milk. Drinking the milk, I thought

132

about Doctor Korczak and the cow. We told the little boy we were playing a game called Whisper so he wouldn't talk or laugh too loud. When we went out the window with our sacks full, the boy wanted to come with us. He cried. We told him we would come back again to visit him, but I knew we could never return to that house.

At first Janina's father did not know she went smuggling with me. He was always sleeping when we slipped quietly out of the room. I think Uncle Shepsel was often awake, but he never said anything. Then came the night we returned, sacks full, and found a lineup happening in the courtyard. Jackboots shouting. Jackdogs snarling. Blinding lights. "Filthy pigs of Abraham!"

We hid our sacks and sneaked behind the last row of people. We crept around until we found the Milgroms. We squeezed in between Uncle Shepsel and Mr. Milgrom. I was shocked to see Mrs. Milgrom standing in line. Her head drooped on her chest. It was a very poor attention.

Mr. Milgrom's hand came down and squeezed Janina's ear. She squeaked.

A nearby Jackboot was shouting. "You smelly animals! You stink! Don't you ever wash!"

I hoped Buffo wasn't there. This was his chance to get me.

A man with a bullhorn was up front. "We know you are doing it! This is your first and last warning! You will be caught! Yes! Yes! And when you are caught you will be shot! If you are lucky! If you are not lucky, we will hang you! Either way, you are dead! One way is slower! More painful! Do you understand!"

"*Jawohl!*" I called out, using the Jackboot word for "yes." No one else spoke.

This time it was my ear that got squeezed. I looked up at Mr. Milgrom. "What is he talking about?"

He whispered, "You. Smugglers. You must stop now."

I did not stop. But I tried to make Janina stop. The next time she followed me into the night I stopped in the courtyard and told her to go back.

"No," she said.

"Your father wants you to stop," I told her. "He'll be mad if they shoot you."

"No."

"They'll hang you."

"No."

"You get in my way. You're a filthy Jew."

"So are you. No."

I could barely see her face in the darkness. I smacked her. This time I didn't give her a chance to smack me back. I pushed her to the ground. She came up flailing at me, and I hit her and pushed her again and hit her again. She was crying. I left her there and walked away. She didn't come after me. She started yelling, "Misha's going to the wall! Misha smuggles! Misha smuggles!"

Out in the street a whistle blew.

I ran back to her. I clamped my hand over her mouth. "Okay," I said, "okay." I yanked her hair. Her yowl echoed in the courtyard. The whistle blew. We ran.

29

We made it to the wall and practically dove through the two-brick hole, but we didn't smuggle that night. I had the idea that as long as we didn't steal food, she was safe. As we passed houses, she kept pestering, "Let's go in there . . . there!"

To distract her, I led her to the merry-go-round. It was deserted and dark. The people were in bed. A streetlight in the distance caught several horses leaping out of the shadows. There was no music, nothing going around, yet I could have sworn they were moving. I looked at the empty spot. I thought of the beautiful black horse, chopped off at the hooves. I thought of the man who turned blue.

We went to the far side, away from the light. We each climbed onto a horse. We pretended we were galloping, racing. Janina kept shouting, "I win!" After a while she came over to my horse and climbed on behind me. She put her arms around my waist. Her chin jutted into my back. "Faster! Faster!"

When I got tired of this, I said, "Do you want to see an angel?"

"What's an angel?" she said.

"I'll show you."

We climbed down from the horse and I took her to the cemetery. The moon was going in and out of clouds. The night sky looked like smoking rubble. It took a while but I finally found it. It towered above us. The wings blotted out much of the sky. "There," I said.

She gazed up, her mouth open. "Angel?"

"It's not a real one," I told her. "It's only made of stone. It's what real ones would look like if you could see them."

"Why can't we see them?"

"Because they hide inside people. There's one inside of you."

"*Inside* me?"

I clamped my hand over her mouth. "Everybody has an angel hiding inside. When you die, your angel comes out. You can die, but not your angel. Your angel never dies."

She looked up at the great wings. "It's too big to fit inside me."

"When it's inside you, it's little," I told her. "When it comes out, it grows, like a balloon." My own mouth was never shy about adding details that the boys had overlooked.

She felt herself all over. She stuck her fingers in her ears, in her nostrils. "I don't feel it." She reached up and pulled my mouth open and tried to peer inside. "I don't see yours." She stomped her foot. "I want to see one!"

"You can't," I told her. But I didn't exactly believe that. I believed that sooner or later I would catch a glimpse of one coming out of a freshly dead body, or just hanging around, reluctant to leave. "They don't live here. They live in Heaven."

"Where's that?"

"I don't know," I said. "Enos says it's right here, on this side of the wall, but I never saw an angel over here. Kuba says it's in Russia. Olek says Washington America."

"What's Washington America?"

"Enos says it's a place with no wall and no lice and lots of potatoes."

Janina reached out and touched the stone foot. Then she smacked it. "I don't like you," she said.

We went home.

I hoped we wouldn't walk into a lineup again. We didn't. But there was something else. Creeping along the shadows toward home, we saw an orange glow beyond a corner and heard a strange sound, like a fierce gust of wind. We sneaked up to the corner for a peek. I couldn't believe what I saw. A man was spouting fire. The fire came gushing out of a hose like burning horsewater and down into a sewer hole in the street.

Enos!

Ferdi!

Olek!

We ran home. I couldn't sleep. At sunrise—Janina was snoring—I raced to the butcher shop ruins. They were there. All of them. I told them what I saw.

Ferdi blew a smoke ring.

Olek said, "Flamethrower."

Enos said, "They're cracking down."

Kuba said, "You sewer rats should come over the wall with me. The sewer stinks."

"They can't watch all the manholes," said Enos. "And the flamethrower only reaches twenty meters."

"It's gorgeous," I said. They all stared at me. I would have stared at myself if I could. I don't know where I got that word. But it was true. When I saw the brilliant orange flame in the night, I saw better than ever before how gray was the world I lived in.

30

I could not stop Janina from following me. And we couldn't eat merry-go-round horses and stone angels. So, soon we were stealing food again. And then something happened, and I was glad it did.

The day was hot. Steamy. Janina and I were down near the entrance to the cemetery, on Gesia Street. We were watching the long parade of body wagons lined up at the gate. The wagons were pulled by men-horses. The bodies were in heaps. The number of them was much higher than I could count at the time. A peppery cloud of flies hovered over the flopped arms and legs. The air buzzed.

Only a few living people came with the wagons. Except for the rags they wore and the fact that they were standing, they looked like the bodies. One old woman held on to an ankle jutting out from a heap. A Flop at the gate collected money. Only the dead got into the cemetery for free.

We heard a commotion. We followed the noise to an intersection of streets. There were Jackboots and Flops and young boys. One of the Flops was Buffo. People were watching. I think they did not want to watch, but Jackboots were pointing guns at them. There was also, in the middle of the square, a pile of onions. I could smell them.

A Jackboot was pulling open the jackets of the boys, and the onions were tumbling out. The boys all seemed to have the same problem: they were hunchbacks. Only the humps in their backs were made of onions.

When all the humps were emptied out, the Jackboot called to the people. "We tell you! Do not smuggle! We tell you!" And the Jackboots and Flops began beating the boys with their clubs, and the boys' hats flew and they were screaming and falling and bleeding among the onions and the people watched and did not move.

I pulled Janina away. "See?" I said. I squeezed her arm. I shook her. "See what happens when you steal food! Do you want that to happen to you?"

She yelled into my face, "I hate you!" She broke loose and ran off.

Good, I thought. *She finally learned her lesson.* And for the rest of that day I thought, *The pest is gone.*

I wanted to make sure, so I told her father. I told him she had been following me, smuggling with me. I told him I could not make her stop, I could not keep her safe. She stood beside me, gaping. Her father's face turned hard and ugly. I thought he would smack her, but he didn't even touch her. He bent down until his face was right in front of hers, like a Jackboot in a lineup. He looked at her as if she were a stranger. He said one word: "No."

Her lip pouted out and quivered. Her great eyes watered. She ran to the mattress and threw herself onto it and huddled into her mother.

When I went out that night, she stayed put. It was getting harder to creep down the stairs in the dark now, as people were sleeping there. More and more people were being trucked into the ghetto. People were living in stairwells and bathrooms and cellars and roofs. I felt my way through the sleeping bodies and

139

waited in the shadows of the courtyard. No one came down after me. At every corner along the way to the two-brick hole, I stopped and looked back. No one followed. I wriggled through the hole and thought: *I'm free!*

The next day, back inside the wall, I was sitting on a curb in the street. I was watching a little girl on the opposite curb lunching on the snot pouring from her nose when I heard a familiar cry: "Fatman! Fatman!"

I ran. Sure enough, there was Janina in the middle of the street, squatting on her haunches, hurling her voice, thumbing her nose at Buffo, taunting him in perfect imitation of me. I saw the gleam in Buffo's eyes as he came clumping after her, spewing flecks of mint, his massive belly bouncing.

Janina screamed and laughed and ran. I fell in beside her, and when we turned a corner I shoved her into an alley, and when Buffo came around I threw stones at him, and I saw his eyes darting about for her and his fingers curling. I couldn't stand the thought of him pulling her into the death balloon of his belly. I remembered Kuba and the funeral in the cemetery. I turned my back on Buffo and pulled down my pants and gave him a moon. I heard his roar, and I had to run while pulling up my pants.

When I finally appeared back in the courtyard, Janina could not stop laughing.

I hated her mimicking me in everything I did. All my talents were useless with her. I could not escape her anymore than I could outrun my shadow. From that day on I stopped tormenting Buffo, only to give her one less part of me to copy.

That night I raided two homes on the other side but got only a few sprouting potatoes and a can of sardines. Once again Janina had stayed behind. I dropped a potato through the open back window of the orphanage and returned to the room, stumbling over sleeping bodies on the stairway.

Lying down in the blackness of the room, I reached out to touch Janina. I felt nothing. I groped around. She wasn't there! I sat up. I had a thought but I couldn't believe it. I sat up until I heard the door squeak open. I lay down. I felt her step over me to her place on the floor. I went to sleep.

I had put two potatoes and the sardines on the table when I came in that night. In the morning, there were three potatoes more plus a pancake.

It went that way night after night: through the wall, into Heaven (thanks to Enos, that's what we were calling the other side of the wall), raiding kitchens, cellars, trash cans— separately. Like a good little girl, Janina was obeying her father: she did not go with me. She went on her own.

Sometimes we passed each other in the shadows. Once, we found ourselves spinning around the revolving door of the blue camel hotel at the same time. We pretended not to see each other. One time we almost bumped heads reaching into the same garbage can.

In the mornings, there on the table, would be our loot. She mixed hers with mine. Every morning Mr. Milgrom thanked me for the food. He never thanked Janina, as he believed she never left the room all night. She never claimed credit.

*   *   *

To stop the smugglers, the Jackboots sent more patrols and more dogs into the ghetto at night. There were gunshots. Screams. The orange glow of flamethrowers. But I wasn't afraid. There was still the darkness. And Buffo seemed to appear only in daylight.

One day we were both very sleepy. It had been harder than usual to find food in Heaven the night before, and day was coming by the time we both made it back to the room. We slept for a while and went outside together. We played pick-up-sticks in the dust of the courtyard and then went wandering about the streets. I was, as always, on the alert for signs of Buffo or the mystery cow, but in time the buzzing of the flies and the warmth of the day took the edge from my attention and made me drowsy. I wobbled into an alleyway and laid myself down. Janina, of course, did the same. Within moments I was sleeping.

Next thing I knew, I jerked awake. Janina was screaming. A barefoot clump of rags was slouching off down the alley. Janina was reaching for her shoe on the ground. "He tried to steal my shoe," she whined.

I laughed. "He thought you were dead."

She yelled after the clump: "I'm not dead!"

As she put her shoe back on, she was staring at me. "What's that?" she said. She was pointing to something.

I looked. It was a brown seed with a spray of white fluff coming out of it. It was clinging to my shirt. And suddenly the word for it was on my tongue, a word I didn't even know I knew. "Milkweed," I said.

She plucked it from my shirt. She held it by the seed up to

142

the light. She dusted her nose with it and giggled. She brushed the fluff across her cheek, closing her eyes. She stood on tip-toes and held it as high as she could and let it go. It sailed toward the sky.

"*That's* my angel," she said.

Then they were all around us, milkweed puffs, flying. I picked one from her hair. I pointed. "Look." A milkweed plant was growing by a heap of rubble.

It was thrilling just to see a plant, a spot of green in the ghetto desert. The bird-shaped pods had burst and the puffs were spilling out, flying off. I cracked a pod from the stem and blew into the silk-lined hollow, sending the remaining puffs sailing, a snowy shower rising, vanishing into the clouds.

31

WINTER

A dead leaf skittered in the moonlight as I wriggled my way through the two-brick hole to the other side. I took off my armband. I knew Janina was somewhere behind me. On this bitterly cold night the streets of Warsaw were almost as deserted as those of the ghetto, but the blue camel hotel was always bright and warm.

As I sailed through the revolving door, I caught a glimpse of red hair in the lobby. I went around again and stopped inside. It was Uri! He was dressed in fine clothes—white shirt, black trousers, shoes. I watched him for a moment. He was emptying ashtrays into a wheeled trash can that he pushed around the lobby. I called out: "Uri!" He didn't hear me. He was heading for a hallway at the back of the lobby. "Uri!"

I ran after him. When I got to the hallway, he was gone. I went down the hallway, peeking into dark rooms. Suddenly I was off my feet and flying into one of them. The door slammed shut. I couldn't see a thing, but I knew it was Uri holding me and whispering into my ear. "What are you doing here?"

"I saw you. Ow!" He was squeezing my arm. "I called you. Didn't you see me? What are you doing here?"

He shook me. "Never mind what I'm doing here. I work in the laundry. If I see you in here again, I'll tell them to shoot

you. My name is not Uri here. You never, *never* call me that."
His hand squeezed my neck. His breath was in my face. "Do
you hear?"

I nodded, choking.

"Never come in here again. Get out. Now!"

The door opened and I was flung into the bright hallway.

Outside on the street, I expected to see Janina. She was usually within sight, following me but pretending she wasn't. I
didn't see her. Something inside me said, *Good*. Something
else said, *I don't like this*.

I disappeared into my usual shadows and alleyways. I did not
seek out new places on this night. I went to familiar, reliable
garbage cans and a few unguarded home pantries, places we
both knew well. I kept expecting to bump into her. I kept
glancing around. She wasn't there.

The moon, as always, had moved halfway across the sky by
the time I was done with my shopping. It was full on this night,
my least favorite kind of moon. Normally, I dashed for the wall
and practically dove through the hole. This time I stopped at
the wall and waited, crouching, in the shadow.

I could not stay long. The wall was patrolled. Nothing but
the patrols moved in Warsaw at this time of night. I kept waiting, hoping to see a tiny fragment of shadow break away and
come running to the wall, to me. Somewhere on the other side
of the wall, a dog barked, a whistle blew. I thought of the other
boys. I hoped they were safe.

Something moved down along the wall. A glint of silver in
the moonlight. A patrol was coming. I stuffed my sack through
the hole, then myself.

145

A minute later I found her. She was near a street corner, standing still, not even trying to hide herself, her sack of food dumped on the ground beside her. I did not want to call out. I approached her quietly from behind. She did not move. She seemed to be looking at something. She was looking up. And then I saw. A body was hanging from the crossbar of a streetlight whose lamp had long since stopped shining. It was hanging by the neck.

I wondered why the hanging body had stopped her. It was not the first she had seen. Death was as familiar to us as life. Even those still breathing, walking—they looked as if they were waiting for someone to tell them they were dead.

So why was my heart hammering my chest? Because the body, I could see now as I stopped beside her, had one arm. It was a boy. It was Olek. A sign was hanging across his chest. In the moonlight it was easy to see the words, but I could not read. Flat on the ground, his shadow was hanging too.

32

The next morning Enos told me what the sign said.

"They'll hang us all," he said.

"Not me," I said. "They can't catch me."

"Not me," said Janina. "They can't catch me."

Enos laughed.

We sat on rocks at the ruins of the butcher shop. No one said anything. Ferdi smoked. Kuba stared at the dust. For once, he had nothing funny to say. Big Henryk bawled. He took off his shoes and pounded the frozen earth with them. He threw away the shoes and bawled some more.

I said, "I saw Uri."

No one looked up.

Janina spat in the dirt. "I hate your angels."

The next day the first snow flurries came. Children held their faces to the sky, trying to catch flakes on their tongues.

I visited the orphanage. Doctor Korczak was teaching the children a song. When he saw me, he said, "Misha, come join us. Sing with us." I stood in the middle of the children and sang the words. After the singing we were each given a cabbage cake and a spoonful of fat. I never saw Doctor Korczak eat. Everyone had shoes. When I left, I walked about the ghetto singing my song in the snowflakes. I saw a boy eating a newspaper.

A voice called, "Misha Pilsudski! Misha Milgrom!"

I recognized the voice but I couldn't believe my ears. I turned. It was Uncle Shepsel. Since the day the Jews paraded into the ghetto, I had not seen Uncle Shepsel outside the room, except for lineups. He was smiling, showing the world his brown teeth. His hand came down on my shoulder. "Misha . . . Misha . . . Is it not a beautiful day?"

I looked around. It seemed like any other day to me. Gray. Up the street a man was banging his head against a stone wall.

But I was an agreeable fellow. "Yes," I said.

"Yes . . . yes . . ." He looked around. He closed his eyes and took a deep breath and stood like that for a while. I thought he had gone to sleep. The head of the man up the street was red, but he was still banging. Uncle Shepsel opened his eyes and smiled down at me. I had seen the same smile in the room lately, as he read the book that had changed him from a Jew to a Lutheran. He removed my cap and mussed my hair. Lice eggs flew like baby snowflakes. He replaced my cap. He nodded dreamily. Suddenly his expression changed. He seemed confused. He looked hard into my face and did not seem to know me. "You go. Every night you go," he said. "Why do you come back?" I did not have an answer. Maybe he found it in my face, for after a while he turned and walked off. Up the street the man was on the ground.

My feet led me back to the room. Mrs. Milgrom was lying on the mattress as usual, facing the wall. She looked the same in every way, and yet I knew at once that she was dead. Mr. Milgrom was sitting on the edge of the mattress. Janina was in his lap. Her face was in his chest and she was crying. Her father rocked her back and forth. When he looked at me, his eyes were shining.

Ever since Mr. Milgrom had made me a member of the family, I had wanted to call Mrs. Milgrom "Mother." I did so once, and she replied, "I'm not your mother." I was confused. By the time I decided to try again, she had turned her back on the room for good. And now she was dead. And Mr. Milgrom's eyes were making me sad. I put my hand on his shoulder, as Doctor Korczak had often done to me. I looked into his shining eyes and I said, "Tata." He took me onto his lap next to Janina, and now I was being rocked back and forth too. I tried to cry like my sister, but I was too busy looking for Mrs. Milgrom's angel.

We sat up all night with the body of Mrs. Milgrom—except for Uncle Shepsel, who went to sleep when he returned to the room. In the morning Mr. Milgrom left and came back with the undertaker. He gave the undertaker a small bottle of white pills. He said he had been saving them for this day. He reached under the mattress and pulled out a little black bowl-shaped piece of cloth. I wondered what it was. He put it on his head. It was a hat.

The undertaker and his two helpers carried Mrs. Milgrom down to the courtyard, where a cart was waiting. Mrs. Milgrom was laid in the cart and covered with a ragged scrap of cabbage-colored wool that had once been a blanket.

The undertaker led the way out of the courtyard. Then came

the helpers pulling the cart. Then came the three of us. Uncle Shepsel stayed back in the room.

We were the smallest parade ever. There were many bodies along the way. I was surprised that we were not picking up some of them. But I was pleased also, because I did not want to see Mrs. Milgrom wind up on the bottom of a heap.

I had never been so slow before. Even when I was not fleeing, I was running or at least walking fast. Everything I did was fast. I forced myself to keep pace with Mr. Milgrom and Janina. He held my hand. I kept telling myself: *My mother is dead in the cart. I must not go faster than her.*

We passed the orphanage. Doctor Korczak stood in the doorway. He put his hands together and closed his eyes and said words. I could not hear them, but I could see them puff from his mouth in the winter air.

Many women passed us going the other way. They all wore coats and wraps of fox and other furs. They looked very sad. Some were crying. They had been ordered to turn in all furs at Stawki Station.

A man went marching past us in the street. He had no shirt or coat on, no shoes or rags on his feet. He made peeping sounds from a silver pipe that he held to his mouth. He waved the pipe in the air and called out: "Children! Children! Come with me! We go to the candy mountain! Follow me! Follow me!"

At the gate to the cemetery on Gesia Street, Mr. Milgrom gave the guard a bottle of pills and we were let in. We went to an empty plot of ground. The undertaker's helpers found shovels and dug a hole. A crow sat nearby on a tilting tombstone.

It stared at me. I thought it spoke to me. In its croaky voice it said the same thing over and over. I could not understand. I left Mrs. Milgrom's side and walked toward the crow. "What?" I called. The crow spoke one last time and flew off.

As they were laying Mrs. Milgrom in her grave, the first bomb fell on the other side of the wall. I felt it in my feet. I looked up. It was raining bombs. The ground was trembling, as if all of the dead had decided to leave their graves at once. The undertaker and his helpers and the cemetery guards all ran. Mr. Milgrom just stood there, staring into the hole.

A bomb exploded several blocks away on our side of the wall. Then more came. Mr. Milgrom looked at us. "Children," he said. He lifted each of us and lowered us into the hole with Mrs. Milgrom. "Cover your eyes." We curled around each other on the scrap of wool at the feet of Mrs. Milgrom. The earth was thumping like a heart. When I peeked upward, I saw Mr. Milgrom sitting on the edge of the grave hole, his feet dangling toward us.

Janina pulled something from her pocket. It was a milkweed pod. She must have plucked it from the plant in the alley. It looked empty. She blew into it. Three or four puffs rose into the air. They sailed up and out of the grave, past Mr. Milgrom and into the rectangle of gray sky and the black falling teardrops of the bombs.

33

When the bombing stopped, we returned home to Uncle Shepsel shouting in the courtyard. "It's the Russians! We're saved!" He danced into the street. "We're saved!"

Uncle Shepsel was the only one dancing.

Upstairs, we found other people in our room. With people being trucked into the ghetto every day, this was happening everywhere. Now it was happening to us.

Janina snapped, "You're in our house." Everyone stared, but no one said anything. Mr. Milgrom pushed his pill cabinet and the table to one side of the room. To the people he said, "You can have the mattress."

I went to find the boys. Enos was standing on top of the butcher shop rubble. He was laughing. The others were staring up at him.

"What's funny?" I said.

"What's funny?" He laughed some more. "Everything! They herd us in here like animals. They build a wall around us. They starve us. They freeze us. They beat us. They shoot us. They hang us. They set us on fire. And then guess what?" He reached down to Big Henryk and rapped him on the head. "Guess what?"

"What?" said Big Henryk.

"I'll tell you what." Enos started laughing again. "The Russians come along and say, 'That's not enough. You Nazis are too easy on them. So we're going to bomb them.' And that's what they do." He threw out his arms. "They bomb us!"

He looked at us all. "You don't think that's the funniest thing you ever heard of?"

No one laughed, not even Kuba.

Funny or not, the bombs kept falling and the winter was cold and the people were hungry. Orphans by the thousands roamed the streets in their rags and boils, slumped in doorways, begging for food, clothing, anything. There was nothing to give them. So they starved and froze and died in the snow, their arms frozen outward, still begging. The children who lived were all scraps and eyes. This was the ghetto: where children grew down instead of up.

I couldn't believe there had been a time when the boys and I had wrestled in piles of food.

One day Janina and I heard a commotion in the courtyard. We looked down from the window. A Jackboot and his girlfriend were standing in the entrance. The man had a bag. He was pulling pieces of bread from the bag and tossing them onto the snow. Every time he tossed a piece ten people pounced on it. The soldier and his girlfriend laughed. They called other couples to come and watch and laugh with them. I saw one girlfriend who did not laugh.

If only lice were food. Every morning we awoke with eyelashes gunked with lice. They made a *pop!* and squirted red when we squeezed them between thumb and fingernail.

Every day the man with the silver pipe marched up and down the streets. "Come to the candy mountain!" Once, I saw a boy stagger after him, but the piper was going too fast.

With the new people in the room, Janina and I could no longer leave our smuggled food on the table. When we returned each night, we slipped food into the coat pockets of Mr. Milgrom and Uncle Shepsel as they slept.

There were seven new people. Five were adults, two were little twin boys. The adults never spoke to Uncle Shepsel or Mr. Milgrom, but the twin boys came to Janina and me when we were playing pick-up-sticks. They tried to play, but they were too little to do it right. They made Janina laugh. She began to leave a piece of potato or onion under their noses at night.

There was even less food now since the bombing by the Russians. It had gone on for many days. Most of the bombs had fallen on Heaven. The clang of the trolleys was gone. The colors were gone, except for the glowing blue line of the camel.

We smuggled every night. On the way over, Janina stayed far behind. Sometimes I turned quickly to catch sight of her, but there were only shadows. It was her game.

Then we had an unexpected holiday.

As I was nearing the hole in the wall one night, I heard a sound. I looked. There was something on the ground. I picked it up. It was a cabbage. A firm, fine one. Suddenly more things were falling at my feet. Sausages and potatoes. By now Janina was with me, scooping them up.

"Somebody is throwing food over the wall," I said in wonder.

We stood there, looking up, but nothing else came down. We ran home with the food, giggling all the way.

The next night we were ready as the food came flying over the wall again. This happened night after night. Tins of sardines and herring. Fruit and babkas of all flavors. More than anything, we loved seeing the astonished faces of Mr. Milgrom and Uncle Shepsel when we returned with our nightly feast.

And then, just as suddenly, the flying food stopped. We were back on our own.

We always met on the other side. If she didn't find me searching for food, she would be waiting for me at the two-brick hole. We always came back through the wall together—me first, then her—ever since the night we found Olek.

Until the night I couldn't fit back through the hole.

First I took off my coat and stuffed it through the hole. I still couldn't get through. I panicked. I tore off my pants and jammed myself into the hole and didn't stop until I was through. I reached back for my pants and re-dressed myself, but Janina was already laughing so hard her cabbages were rolling across the ground.

The next day at the butcher shop I found a good bone among the charred bricks and handed it to Big Henryk and said, "Beat me."

Big Henryk was confused. I knew he wouldn't understand.

"I'm getting too big," I said to Enos. I lay on the ground on my back. I raised the bottoms of my feet to Big Henryk. "Beat my feet," I told him. "I need to stop growing."

Enos laughed. "Beat him," he said. "If you don't, I will."

Big Henryk's first wallop sent me skidding over the frozen

ground like a sled on ice. Everyone laughed. Enos pushed against my shoulders to keep me from sliding. He told Big Henryk to beat away.

Big Henryk was beating away on the soles of my feet when I heard the moo. We all heard it. I couldn't believe it. All along I had been on the lookout for the cow. I so wanted to please Doctor Korczak. And now here it was, plain to hear as a Flop's whistle. But it didn't sound right.

It was nearby. We ran to the street. To a courtyard. There it was, galloping across a balcony, a flaming, fiery cow, screaming while a Jackboot behind it laughed and the flamethrower retched more fire until the cow plunged through the railing and sailed through the air, flames flapping like wings to the ground.

One person ran across the courtyard to the burning cow. And then it was mobbed.

34

"This year you will celebrate with us," said Mr. Milgrom.

He meant the holiday called Hanukkah. It was the first Jewish word I had learned. He had wanted to include me the year before, but Mrs. Milgrom would not allow it. "No," she had said, groaning from her mattress. "He is not a Jew. I am not his mother." "She is not herself," Mr. Milgrom had said. Still, I was not allowed. For eight nights I had sat in a corner and watched.

Now it was Hanukkah time again, and Mrs. Milgrom was gone and Uncle Shepsel had walked outside, being a Lutheran now, and I was in. On the first day Mr. Milgrom told me the story of Hanukkah. How long ago the Greeks tried to destroy everything Jewish. ("See, this is not the first time.") How the Jews were outnumbered and had no chance against the Greeks but beat them anyway. How the Jews celebrated by lighting an oil lamp. But the celebration would have to be short because there was only enough oil to last for one day. And then a miracle happened. The oil lasted for eight days.

"And so Hanukkah is eight days when we remember that time, and we remember to be happy and proud to be Jews and that we will always survive. This is our time. We celebrate ourselves. We must be happy now. We must never forget how to be happy. Never forget."

"Happy." I had not heard that word since Mr. Milgrom spoke it at the last Hanukkah. I asked him the question that had been on my mind since then. "Tata, what is happy?"

He looked at me and at the ceiling and back to me. "Did you ever taste an orange?" he said.

"No," I said, "but I heard of them. Are they real?"

"Never mind." He stared at me some more. "Did you ever—" He stopped and shook his head.

After more staring, he said, "Were you ever cold, and then you were warm?"

I thought of sleeping with the boys under the braided rug: cold, then warm. "Yes!" I blurted. "Was that happy?"

He smiled. "That was happy."

I felt again the cuddled tent of warmth. Sometimes I would stick my nose out to better feel the warmth on the rest of me. "Under the rug."

"No," he said. He tapped my chest. "Happy is here." He tapped his own chest. "Here."

I looked down past my chin. "Inside?"

"Inside."

It was getting crowded in there. First angel. Now happy. It seemed there was more to me than cabbage and turnips.

I looked at Janina sitting potato-faced on the floor. She hadn't smiled since the burning cow. "Janina does not have happy."

He squeezed my shoulder. He smiled sadly. "No."

Mr. Milgrom took the silver candleholder from the pill cabinet and lit the first of eight candles. The twins came over to stare at the flame. The other new people stayed on their side of the room.

Gunshots echoed in the streets as Mr. Milgrom said words

over the candle flame. The flame gave a faint yellow tint to his frozen breath. Then he sang a song. "Sing, Janina," he said, but Janina only gave a grunt or two. Then he pulled Janina and me to our feet, and the twins also, and he made us all hold hands and we danced in a circle while Mr. Milgrom sang and the candle flame quivered and somebody screamed in the night.

The smile never left Mr. Milgrom's face. I copied his smile as best I could. Janina's shoulders slumped and her shoes dragged across the floor.

I wondered if the orphans were dancing in a circle.

Then Mr. Milgrom took something, and another something, from his coat pocket. They were wrapped in newspaper. He gave one to Janina, one to me. I tore mine open. It was a comb. I couldn't believe it. I remembered the canister full of combs in the barbershop. I remembered Uri combing my hair. Now I had my very own!

I threw off my cap and sank the comb like a spade into my hair. It stuck. I pulled. I couldn't move it. I dropped the comb and began tearing apart the thatch of hair with my fingers. I tried the comb again. Using all my strength, I was finally able to pull the comb through my hair. I could feel the lice and their eggs peppering the back of my neck. I heard them ticking onto the floor.

In the light of the candle, I combed and combed and combed my hair. Not until the next day did I notice that Janina's gift was still wrapped in newspaper.

"You're not going to open it?" I said.

She pouted. "No."

So I opened it. It was a comb just like mine. I gave it to her.

She threw it on the floor. I picked it up and began combing her curly brown hair. "See?" I said. "Doesn't that feel good? And it's better than picking out lice with our fingers."

She did not answer. She did not smile. She did not stop me from combing.

On the second day of Hanukkah, when Mr. Milgrom went for the silver candleholder, it was gone. Mr. Milgrom seemed surprised, but I wasn't. In my world, things existed to be stolen. With the other family in the room, everyone knew who did it. And why. If you knew who to deal with, things could be traded for money, and money could be traded for food.

Mr. Milgrom accused no one. He simply looked out the window and said loud enough for all in the room to hear: "What a shame when Jew will steal from Jew."

He found a candle stub and lit the tiny wick with a match. He looked at Janina and me. "Who will be the menorah?" The menorah was the candleholder.

"I will!" I said.

He gave me the candle. He made for it a collar of newspaper so the hot wax would not drip on my hand. I stood at attention and held my arms out and did my best to imitate a menorah. Mr. Milgrom said the words and sang. I asked him if I could sing the song I learned at Doctor Korczak's orphanage. His eyes glistened in the light from my candle. "Yes! Yes!" So I sang my song—a singing candleholder—and Mr. Milgrom and the twins danced in a circle and laughed. Janina refused to get up from the floor.

So the days of Hanukkah went. When the candle burned

away, Mr. Milgrom struck a match and said that maybe it would last for eight days, like the oil in the story. But it burned away before he finished speaking. "So," he said, "we ourselves will be the candle flames." He put his hands on his chest. "Feel your hearts, how warm they are." And I did, I could feel my heart getting warm, I could feel the flame in my chest as we danced in a circle.

Each night I went out for food, but Janina stayed behind. She never left the room. She never spoke. She even stopped complaining. I combed her hair for hours each day, but I could not comb a smile onto her face. I also was losing my happy.

Then an idea came to me.

Although Janina did not like her comb, I knew of something she would like very much. Almost every time she ate I heard her mutter, "I wish I had a pickled egg." I knew about pickled herring but not pickled eggs. I thought: *I'll find an egg and a pickle*.

There was only one day of Hanukkah left. That night when I went to the other side, I forgot about everything else. I could not remember seeing an egg in my smuggling searches, but then I hadn't been looking for eggs. I knew eggs were kept in cool places, so I looked in iceboxes and basements. I went to all my best houses plus the blue camel hotel and found not a single egg.

As for pickles, I was hoping for the fat, juicy kind that Uri used to eat, but the best I could do was a jar of pickle spears in someone's pantry. I was traveling light this night, so I just took a couple of spears from the jar and put them in my pocket. Now all I needed was an egg.

It had begun to snow. I lurked down alleyways, jiggling strange doors and windows, trying to get in somewhere. There were more ruins now, after the Russians' bombing. Parts of Heaven were beginning to look like the ghetto. At last I found an egg, not in a great house but in a shoemaker's shop. And not in an icebox but sitting on a scrap of leather on a workbench. I cradled the egg in my hand. I knew how fragile they were. I could already hear Janina's joyful squeal.

On the way back, out on the street, I heard a whistle blast. I thought nothing of it. The Jackboots were after someone. The whistle kept getting louder, and then a shouting voice: "Jude! Jude!" I didn't understand. No one ever stopped me over here. I ran. A second voice was shouting. Snowflakes pelted my face. I kept my fingers loose about the egg.

I could not run in a straight line, for there were craters in the streets from the bombing. And I could not lead them to the hole in the wall. I darted into an alley and into the shadows and deep into a heap of rubble. I crouched, panting, pressing the cold, smooth egg to my lips. The shouts and whistles grew faint. I waited for a long time. The snow piled on my hat and collar. I could smell the pickles in my pocket. I warmed the egg with my breath.

The sky was turning from black to gray when I made my way back to the two-brick hole. I reached to the other side and laid the egg in the snow and wriggled after it. I had been having no problems getting through lately. Big Henryk's walloping must have worked.

The moment I returned to the ghetto side I realized why the Jackboots had been after me. I had forgotten to take off my armband. I had been announcing to all of Warsaw: *Look! I'm a Jew! Escaped from the ghetto!* It was a wonder they hadn't noticed me sooner.

Darkness, my friend, was leaving. I had to hurry. I ran. Dashing around a corner, I tripped over a body half hidden in the snow and went sprawling on the sidewalk. The egg flew from my hand. At first I was happy for the pillow of snow, but when I picked up the egg I saw in the dim light that the shell was cracked. I was heartbroken. All the dangers it had survived, only to come to this.

And then I noticed that it was only cracked, not broken apart. There was no yellow seeping into the snow. I didn't understand. An egg that cracked but didn't break. It was a miracle!

I ran the rest of the way, veering around bodies. Mr. Milgrom was already awake when I got home. Janina was sleeping. I showed him the egg and the pickle spears. "For Janina," I whispered. "Happy."

He looked at the egg and pickle spears, but he looked longer at me.

"Look at the egg," I said. "It doesn't break. Is it a miracle?"

He studied the egg. He held it to his ear and shook it. He nodded. "No," he whispered. "The miracle is you. The egg is hard-boiled. It will not break."

A hard-boiled egg. This was new to me. I hoped Janina would like it.

That night I gave it to her. Her eyes bulged like bird's eggs. She peeled off the shell and shoved the whole egg into her mouth. She closed her eyes and made little sounds as she ate it.

"Wait," I said. "Pickles." I held them out. "Pickled egg."

She waved the pickles away. "Pickled eggs are purple," she mumbled through the mush in her mouth. The twins were staring. Their teeth were going up and down with hers.

When she finished eating the egg, she hugged her father and said, "Thank you."

"Thank Misha," he said. "It was his idea. He found it on the other side."

She hugged me. I was surprised she could squeeze so hard.

Uncle Shepsel returned. He came to the room only to eat and sleep now. He believed that the less time he spent with Jews, the more Lutheran he became. But even Lutherans get hungry, and when he came in the door he sniffed the air and said, "Pickles."

To my surprise, Mr. Milgrom took a pickle spear from his pocket and gave it to Uncle Shepsel.

As for me, I had been awake too long. I lay down. I felt a comb in my hair . . . combing . . . combing . . .

35

SPRING

"What's that?" Janina said. She went to the window. The twins ran after her.

We were in the room. It was day. There were voices outside the window. I joined the others.

In the courtyard below, children were singing. They sounded more like crows than like children. When they sensed we were watching from above, they turned their faces up to us, all rags and eyes.

"Why are they singing?" I said.

Mr. Milgrom's voice came over my shoulder. "They are hungry. They are singing for food."

"We have no food," I said.

This was true. When Janina and I returned from Heaven each night—she was going out with me again—we dropped something through the window of Doctor Korczak's orphanage and brought the rest straight home and ate it at once.

"Come away from the window, children," said Mr. Milgrom.

The singing in the courtyard went on for a while, then it went away.

The flies were always singing. The days were warm and the bodies were cold and the flies were singing and drinking at the eyes and boils of the children. No one took from the bodies under the newspapers, as there were no clothes left to take, no shoes, only rags. I believed I saw angels lurking behind the eyes of the living, waiting. Angels and crows passed each other, one leaving, the other coming.

Every day a parade of body wagons backed up at the Gesia Street gate of the cemetery.

Smugglers hung like sad fruits from lampposts with signs around their necks.

The piper marched up and down the streets and blew his silver flute and cried out, "Come to the candy mountain!"

On Sundays the Jackboots came with their girlfriends to pinch their noses and take pictures and toss pieces of bread to us pigeons. One soldier made the others laugh: he wore a clothespin on his nose.

Food was harder and harder to find, even in Heaven. Sometimes all I could find was green bread. Sometimes there was nothing in a garbage can but drippings of fat in the bottom. I had no container, so I scooped two handfuls and returned with that. The others ate the fat from my hands.

Even with smuggled food, Janina had gotten thinner and thinner. Her face had become as thin as a fox's. While the rest of her became smaller, her eyes grew larger.

In other ways Janina was her old self again, chattering, complaining, shadowing me everywhere I went, in everything I did. She made me self-conscious. I hesitated to do things that had always come naturally. I had stopped harassing Buffo so that Janina would also stop, but it didn't work. In fact, she went even further. She became a gnat in the nose of every Flop she saw. She called them names. She threw stones. She sneaked up behind them and whacked them on the backs of their knees with a metal pipe.

I smacked her. I shouted at her. But I could not change her. I could not understand her moods, her outbursts. I mostly accepted the world as I found it. She did not. She smacked me back and kicked me. In time I found my own best way to deal with her. On many days I went off to a favorite bomb crater and lowered myself into it and licked traces of fat from between my fingers and closed my eyes and remembered the good old days when ladies walked from bakeries with bulging bags of bread.

36

One minute I was walking alone—I was heading for the bomb crater—and the next minute someone was beside me. I gave a yelp. "Uri!" He had not been around in a long time. I hugged him. He pushed me away.

"Shut up," he said. "Just listen." He smacked me on the back of the head. "Are you listening?"

"Yes," I said.

"Get out," he said.

"Get out?"

He wore a blue-and-white armband just like mine.

"I'm not going to say it again. Get. Out."

I was confused. "Get out of where?"

"Out of the ghetto. Out of Warsaw. Out of everywhere. Just get out. Go. And don't look back."

There were no scabs or boils on Uri's face. He wore clothes. Shoes.

A hollow-eyed, rag-draped skeleton appeared before us. I could not tell if it was a boy or a girl. It held out its hand. Uri pulled a fat pickle from his pocket. He bit off a piece, took the piece from his mouth, and gave it to the hand. We walked on.

"Why?" I said.

"Deportations," he said. "They're going to begin soon. They're clearing out the ghetto."

"Deport——?"

"Deportations. They're going to get rid of all of you. Take you away on trains."

This sounded good to me. "Where?" I said. "Russia? Washington America?"

He curled his fingers around my neck. He squeezed. "I don't know. You don't *want* to know. Whatever you do, do *not* get on a train. Do *not* be here when the trains come. Just go. Get out. Run. Don't stop running." He looked at the sky. "Ever."

I looked at the sky with him, but nothing was there.

He stared at me. "I never asked you—how do you get to the other side?"

I told him about the two-brick hole.

He wagged his head. He almost grinned. "You little turd. I knew you'd be good for something."

"Remember when I saw you in the blue camel hotel?" I said excitedly.

He bounced a knuckle off my forehead. "You didn't see me anywhere, you hear? You never saw me. You don't know me." Another knuckle. "You understand?"

I nodded, but I did not understand.

"I have to go," he said. "Here." He gave me the rest of the pickle. He stepped back. He stared at me up and down. He wagged his head. He looked sad. "Darker than ever." He spit on his finger and rubbed my cheek. "Before you go, find some water and wash your face." He reached into a rubble of bricks and pulled out a handful of white dust. "See this? Rub your face with it. Your hands." He washed my hands in the dust. They became whiter than his. "See? Before you go"—pointing to my armband—"take off that thing." He grabbed my hair and

169

shook my head till I was dizzy. "Do not look at anyone. Do not stop for anything. You are not a Jew. You are not a Gypsy. You are nobody." He slapped my face. "Say it."

"I am nobody."

He let me go. He backed off. His red hair was cut so short it was just a tinge of rust creeping out of his cap. He turned and walked away. He came back. He squeezed my neck. "Tell no one but the boys," he said. He looked about. "How are they? Are they all right?"

"Not Olek," I said. "Olek is hanged. With a sign." Uri stared at me. "They smuggle, like me. But not through the hole. They're too big."

Uri looked at the sky for a long time. He closed his eyes. He looked back to me. He reached into his pocket and handed me something. "Here." He walked away for good.

It was a piece of candy. The chocolate coat was melting. I ate it. It was a buttercream with a hazelnut heart.

I went straight to the boys at the butcher shop ruins. I told them I had seen Uri. "He says we must go."

Kuba laughed. "Go? Go where?"

"Out of the ghetto," I said. "Out of everywhere. Run. Run forever!"

Kuba and Ferdi laughed. Enos did not. "Why?" he said.

"Deportation."

The boys looked at one another.

"What's that mean?" said Ferdi.

"I don't know," said Enos. But I could tell that he did.

Big Henryk boomed: "Run!"

*   *   *

I saved the pickle for my family. As they chewed the pieces, I said, "We must go." I said it in a whisper so the new people in the room would not hear.

"What are you talking about?" said Uncle Shepsel.

"Uri says the trains are coming to take us away. He says we have to run."

"Who is Uri?" said Mr. Milgrom.

"Uri is my friend."

"Your friend is cuckoo," said Uncle Shepsel. "Why would they take you anywhere? They already have you like pigs in a pen. What else can they do to you? And I say 'you'"—he pointed to each of us—"because I am no longer one of you." He licked pickle juice from his lip. "I am a Lutheran. Everyone knows. I have nothing to fear. I am only thinking of you"—he jabbed his book in Mr. Milgrom's face—"with your Hanukkahs and stubbornness. *You.*"

Janina pulled on her father's sleeve. "I want to go away on the train, Tata."

Mr. Milgrom patted her hand. "There will be no train. Uncle Shepsel is right. There is nothing else they can do to us."

37

SUMMER

Janina was the first to hear it. We had just wriggled through the hole back into the ghetto. My pockets were stuffed with chunks of rotten cabbages.

"What's that?" she said.

We listened.

In the black distance there was a faint sound of metal clanking, screeching.

"I don't know," I said.

She yelped. "It's the trains!"

She ran. She ran stupidly, down the middle of the street, ignoring the shadows. Onions bounced from her pockets. I ran after her. The clanking and screeching became louder.

"Janina! Stop!" I tried to shout without shouting. Curfew began when the sun went down. Nighttime was dangerous for everyone, not just smugglers.

I caught her. I held her by the arms as she tried to kick me. I wanted to hit her, but I was afraid to let go. "They'll shoot you, you stupid girl." I felt her shoulders slump. She relaxed. She was giving up. I let go. She turned suddenly and raised up on her tiptoes and bashed her forehead into my nose. I howled. Tears leaped to my eyes. When I finally managed to see, she was gone.

"Good," I whispered. "Stupid girl." I threw a stone. I shouted as loud as I could: "Stupid girl!"

I tried to go home. I tried to sit in the shadows and wait for her to come back. In the end all I could do was start walking toward the noises in the night. They were coming from Stawki Station, the railroad yard just on the other side of the ghetto wall.

I had long since discovered that the two-brick hole I used nightly was not the only one in the wall. Near the Stawki Street gate there was another. I wriggled through it and found myself once again outside the wall. I saw that there was not one train, but many. Thick, yellow light came from lamps hung high on a forest of poles. Locomotives huffed and whistled and blew steam from their wheels. Endless lines of boxcars vanished into the blackness. Jackboots and Jackdogs flashed from the shadows.

Uri was right.

I found Janina sitting on a collapsed smokestack. I could not help myself. I climbed up beside her.

We watched a train come in and line up with the others.

"Where will they go?" she said, never taking her eyes from the trains. "Where will they take us?"

"You don't want to know," I said.

"Do you know?"

"Yes," I lied. "But I'm not telling you." Punishing her.

We watched some more.

She said, "I know where they're going."

"Where?" I said.

She nodded like her father did when he was saying something important. "They're going to the candy mountain."

173

*   *   *

We said nothing of the trains the next day. We didn't have to. Everyone in the ghetto knew. The words were in the air, buzzing with the flies:

"Trains . . ."

"Deportations . . ."

"Stawki Station . . ."

"Why . . ."

"Where . . ."

Uncle Shepsel became more and more agitated. He wagged his book at the new people. He ranted at the people on the stairway. He called down from the window to the courtyard: "Jews! Repent! It is not too late! Come with me! Save yourselves!"

At the butcher shop ruins, Enos laughed and laughed. He stood on a pile of bricks and spread his arms and shouted: "They're doing it! They're really doing it!"

The piper marched in the streets.

Sounds of singing came through the open windows of the orphanage.

All eyes and ears turned toward Stawki Station. Even the morning corpses seemed to be listening.

Two nights after we first saw the trains, as we returned from the garbage cans of Heaven, we heard the sounds. Gunshots. Whistles. Screams. Snarling dogs. When we came to the two-brick hole, we peeked through, our heads pressed together, one eye apiece. People were going by, many of them, down the middle of the street. Everyone carried a suitcase. My first stupid thought was *Parade!* Then I saw the Jackboots poking them with rifles and the dogs lunging and snapping. The peo-

174

ple went by so slowly. Their feet seemed to slide along the street, not walk. They did not look like they were going to the candy mountain. I thought they would never pass.

The next day the streets were empty.

Voices in the stairway, in the courtyard, said: "There is a quota. The trains must take five thousand Jews every day."

Voices: "Ten thousand."

Voices: "Until—"

And then someone said: "Resettlement."

What did he mean? Resettlement? What resettlement?

"They have had enough of us here," the someone said. "They are sick of us. They are kicking us out. They are sending us to the East. To resettlement. We will have our own villages. No one but Jews!"

The word "resettlement" took the place of the word "deportation."

"Still," said Uncle Shepsel, "it is better not to be a Jew in the first place."

And the Jackboots came in the day and the night, and the whistles blew. One block, one street, at a time.

Sliska Street.

Panska Street.

Twarda Street.

Every day, every night, the slow gray parades shuffled toward Stawki Station.

The people on the stairway muttered: "Resettlement . . . resettlement . . ."

"We will be free!"

175

"I will mend shoes again!"

"We will eat!"

The people looked into each other's eyes and nodded and said, "Yes . . .yes . . ." Still, they did not go outside. The streets remained empty. Except for the piper.

Sometimes when Janina and I climbed down through the people on the stairway at night, a voice would say, "Don't go. You'll miss the resettlement."

Ceglana Street.

Chlodna Street.

One day Mr. Milgrom said to me, "Stay close to Janina, wherever you go. Every second. Day and night." His hand was on my shoulder.

I was shocked. Not that he knew she went out with me at night but that he was allowing her to do so.

There was one thing Mr. Milgrom did not know: how much his daughter loved the trains. Every night when we crawled back through the hole to the ghetto, she ran for the courtyard. She dumped her food under a porch where she could get it later and ran off to the hole in the wall near the Stawki Street gate and squirted herself back to the other side. I remembered Mr. Milgrom's orders. I had no choice but to follow.

Night after night we did this. We stood at the end of the fallen smokestack and stared at the trains coming and going. The parades of people climbing into the boxcars. The screech of wheels. The clack of dogs' teeth. The locomotives coughing like dying Jews.

In the days I went to the butcher shop ruins. But the boys were disappearing one by one. "Where's Ferdi?" I asked. "Where's Kuba?" No answer. Had they taken Uri's advice? Did they run away? Were they on the other side of the wall, running? Were they hanging from lampposts with signs around their necks? Were they in the sewers? Had Buffo found them?

Ferdi.

Kuba.

Enos.

One by one.

Until only Big Henryk was left, clumping after the piper. I saw Jackboots pointing at them.

No one came to take pictures anymore.

All day. All night. Parades of people.

One day I was dozing in the milkweed alley when Janina came calling: "Misha! . . . Misha!" She grabbed my hand and pulled me out to the street. The orphans were going by. They were marching. Their heads were high and they were singing the song I had learned. I sang along with them. Not one was dressed in rags. Everyone wore shoes. Doctor Korczak led the way. He marched as straight as a Jackboot. He wore a hat with a little red feather. We stood there until I could no longer see them, no longer hear them.

Libelta Street.

Walowa Street.

Gesia Street.

38

And then the old man was there.

It was strange. He was not there, and then suddenly he was. He did not even have rags on his feet. One eye was the color of milk. It never blinked.

"I have come back," he said. We were gathered around him in the courtyard. "I am here to tell you. I escaped. I saw. There is no resettlement."

Someone called: "Of course there is resettlement. We go to villages in the East. They are waiting for us."

The man repeated, "There is no resettlement. It is a lie."

"*You* lie!" another someone called.

"Look!" someone else called, waving a piece of paper. "This is a postcard from my brother. He says he is doing fine. Listen. 'We are doing fine. We are happy in our new village. We hope to see you soon.'"

"Lies," said the old man. He did not shout. We had to strain to hear him. He looked and he sounded as if he wanted to sleep. "It is a trick. Your brother is dead."

There was a shriek.

Many shouted at once at the old man.

"Go away!"

"Go away!"

Only when the shouting died down did we know that the old man was saying more: ". . . fences that fry . . . prison coops . . . ovens . . . never stop . . . ashes fall like snow . . ."

There was silence.

Someone said, "Ovens? Are they baking pies for us?"

Laughter.

"Ovens for what?" came another voice.

The old man raised his head. His milky eye turned to the speaker. "For you."

Silence again, and then a louder burst of laughter and jeers.

"You are crazy, old man!"

"We have postcards!"

The old man wobbled. I leaned my shoulder into his hip to hold him up. Above me I heard his ragged breathing. The people waited for him to say more, but he only turned and walked away.

A voice, Uncle Shepsel's, cried out: "Jews! Repent! It is not too late!"

A day after the old man spoke in the courtyard, Mr. Milgrom whispered to me in a corner of the room. "When you and Janina go out tonight, I want you to stay on the other side. I want you to run away. Don't come back. Keep Janina with you. Take her hand."

First Uri, now my father.

"Janina wants to go on the train," I told him. "She wants to go to the candy mountain."

Mr. Milgrom's eyes slowly closed. Like Janina's, they had become enormous, as if to hold his sadness. "There is no candy mountain," he said.

At that moment I knew. The old man in the courtyard had been telling the truth. And I understood why Mr. Milgrom had not forbidden Janina to go out. He knew that when the parade to the trains came by, a child might be safer away from home.

He stared into my eyes. He gripped my forearm. "Take her hand. Keep her with you. Make her go. Take off your armbands and run. Run until daylight. Then hide. Run at night." He squeezed my arm so hard I would have thought he was trying to hurt me if I hadn't known better. "Do not bring back food tonight. Do not return. Run. *Run*."

That night Mr. Milgrom was not sleeping when we got up to go. He pressed us into himself for a long time. I think he was crying. He whispered words in our ears that I did not understand and let us go.

When we got to the other side that night, I took Janina's hand as Mr. Milgrom had told me. At first she said nothing. When she saw we were not stopping at garbage cans, she planted her feet and said, "Where are we going?"

"I don't know," I said. "We're just going."

She yanked her hand out of mine and stomped off.

I went after her and grabbed her hand back. "Tata said to come with me."

"Where?"

"Away. Now run."

I started to run, pulling her along. She jammed her heels into the sidewalk and screamed and kicked me. Just when I thought she was finished with me, she spat on my shirt and stomped on my foot. I screamed. She ran off.

We did not go to the trains that night. We returned to the room with brown cabbages and fat. Mr. Milgrom was still awake. He squeezed my arm and shook me. "What did I tell you?" I could not see his face in the darkness, but his voice was furious. I think he wanted to smack me. Then he pressed us again into himself.

This is how it went for a number of nights. Mr. Milgrom told me—and then the both of us—not to return, Janina refused to obey; we returned to the furious voice and the smack that never came.

Zamenhof Street.
Mila Street.
Lubecki Street.

And then one night we could not come back.

39

Our pockets were stuffed with dried herring. Janina smelled like salt and fish. When we came near our two-brick hole, we saw lights and people. We hid in the shadows and waited. Finally, the lights went out and the people left. We ran to the hole. It wasn't there. Only an unbroken flatness of brick.

We crept along the wall. We went into Stawki Station. Boxcar doors were clanking, swallowing whole parades of people. Aching to get back to the ghetto, we looked for the Stawki Station hole that we had been coming through to see the trains. It too was gone.

"There's other holes," I said. All night long we darted from shadow to shadow along the never-ending wall, dodging Jackboot guards, searching for a way into the ghetto. There were guards and lights and flat brick wall, but no holes. We heard gunshots and screams coming from the ghetto. Dogs barking. Glow of flamethrowers. Janina became more and more agitated. Whenever she heard a gunshot, she piped, "Tata!" She kicked at the wall.

"He's all right," I told her. I hugged her.

The sky was gray, the stars were fading, when we got back to where we started. Daylight was coming, and we were stuck in Heaven.

I found white dust at the base of the wall. I washed my face and hands in it. Janina laughed. She smacked me with a dried fish, then we ate it. We slept on the ground in the merry-go-round park. We woke at noon and walked about the city. I remembered Uri's words. I told Janina, "Don't look guilty."

"What's guilty?" she said.

"I forget," I said. "Just don't look it."

I reached into her pocket and pushed her crumpled armband deeper out of sight.

We wandered the streets, among the people and bomb craters, chewing dried fish. We made a game—who could look less guilty? We laughed. We said hello to people. We ran back to the merry-go-round to ride the horses, but the horses were still. I kept listening for the tootling music, but all I heard were gunshots from the other side of the wall.

When night returned, we approached the wall. And I realized how stupid I was. What had I been thinking? Were the holes going to come back? Was the wall going to be lower than last night? I wished we had Big Henryk's shoulders to climb on. I tried to think, tried to think. Suddenly Janina ran to the wall and cupped her hands about her mouth and yelled with all her might: "Tataaaa!" I tackled her and rolled us into the shadows as a Jackboot down the wall turned.

Just to be doing something, we began another tour around the wall. When we came to Stawki Station, where it was always daytime, with the lights and trodding people and clanking boxcars, I suddenly knew what to do. The Stawki Street gate in the wall was open. People were parading through. I grabbed her hand, pulled her along. We crouched behind a shed near the gate.

Jackboots with dogs guarded both sides of the gate. The

people slumped along with their suitcases, heads hung low, as if they did not know the teeth of the dogs were snapping into their faces.

I did not bother to give Janina instructions. Why should I? She copied everything I did. I dashed for the parade of people. I plunged into them. I lost myself among their legs. While they headed for the trains, I groped and shouldered in the opposite direction. They paid no more attention to me than to the dogs. When I sensed I had passed through the gate to the ghetto side, I broke sharply to my right, popped out of the parade, and bolted. There were dogs and shouts behind me, then gun-shots—my first prayer plucked at my lips: *No flamethrowers, please*—but by then there were shadows and rubble and I was tucked into a pocket of blackness like a rat.

I did not know if she was with me until my own heart and lungs calmed down. Then I could hear her panting beside me. When no one seemed about, we ran for home.

I knew the news was bad as we raced up the steps. There were no bodies to hurdle: the squatters were gone. Our door was open. Moonlight misted from the window like winter breath. The room was empty. The table and chair were over-turned. The pill cabinet was smashed. Janina cried out. She flung herself onto the floor and into the corners. She scrubbed the shadows with her body, hoping he was only hiding, not gone. She whimpered along the walls. "Tata . . . Tata . . ." She ran to the window. "Tataaaa!"

Where was Uncle Shepsel? I expected him to arise any moment in the middle of the room and declare: "I tried to warn them! The Jews! They would not listen!"

Then I saw it, in the moonlight on the floor: the book of Lutherans.

Janina knocked me aside as she ran from the room and down the steps. I ran after her, across the courtyard, down the middle of the moonlit streets to Stawki Station.

The endless parade was still shuffling through the gate into the yellow light. I lost her as she plunged into the people. I did likewise. The dogs gasped on their leashes, but no one tried to stop us. On the other side of the wall, I made my way from side to side of the parade, bouncing off suitcases, searching for her. Whistles shrieked. Boxcar doors screamed. Dogs yapped and snarled. Jackboots and dogs and bayonets threw gigantic, jerking shadows on the ground.

I kept working my way backward through the parade so I would not be carried to the boxcars. I peeked out from the people, searching, keeping myself hidden among the shuffling legs and suitcases.

Then I saw her. Or did I? Was it really her? How could I be sure? It was four or five boxcars down the line. Everything— the people's heads, the straining dogs, the roofs of the boxcars—was in black silhouette against the sickly light. She was a shadow cut loose, held above the other shadows by a pair of Jackboot arms. She was thrashing and screaming above the silent masses. I could not make out her words, but the sound of the voice was hers, and I was running, breaking from the parade and running toward her. And then the arms came forward and she was flying, Janina was flying over the shadow heads and the dogs and soldiers, her arms and legs turning slowly. She seemed so light, so right for the air—I thought:

She's happy! I thought she would sail forever like a milkweed puff on an endless breeze, and I was running and wishing I could fly with her, and then she was gone, swallowed by the black maw of the boxcar, and even as I felt the hot breath of the dog, I could hear the rumble and the boxcar door clanking shut.

I tried to run to her, but the dog wouldn't let me go, and then the dog was gone and a boot came swinging and I was kicked so hard I popped off the ground. When I landed, a club pounded my shoulders and I was kicked again and the Jackboot was dragging me by the hair and there was laughing and clacking of Jackdog teeth. The Jackboot flung me against a wall. I saw his hand go to his holster. I saw the gun come out and point between my eyes. "Die, piglet!" *The voice.* I looked up. The red hair. The face. "Uri!" I cried, and the gun went off.

40

My nose tickled. My cheek. I brushed away the tickles. They came back. Snips of buzzing. I opened my eyes. White clouds sailing across a blue sky. Darting spots. Flies.

Something was ringing. My ear hurt. My arm hurt. Everything hurt.

I was wet. I was in water. I sat up. I was in a puddle of water in a ditch. I started to climb out of the ditch and fell back. The ringing would not stop. I looked at my arm, where the teeth of the dog had shaken me. The gash was crusty, like dark red bread. Flies danced over it. I stared at them. They were busy.

I put my hand to my ear, the one with the missing earlobe. I felt a crusty lump but not much more. I sat back and closed my eyes and listened to the ringing.

Janina!

I scrambled up from the ditch. Stawki Station was empty. No Jackboots. No Jews. The trains were gone. The gate was closed.

I headed for the empty tracks. I felt dizzy. Then I was waking up on the ground. I tried again. The world wobbled. I saw something in the hard dirt. I reached to pick it up and got dizzy and fell on my head. I cried out and went to sleep. When I opened my eyes, it was right there. A black shredded scrap.

187

Her shoe. That I had seen my face in. I would have known it anywhere. I ran my fingertips over it. I smiled. I picked it up and picked myself up and wobbled on.

I came to the edge of the platform. I sat down, my feet dangling toward the tracks below. The ringing was loud. I felt dizzy again. When I woke up, I was on the tracks, the shoe in my fist.

The tracks curved out of the station. I started to walk. I walked out of the station yard, out of the world. The tracks came to a point in the sky.

41

I came to a boy. He was throwing stones down the track. A black-and-white dog was with him. When the dog saw me it came running. I was afraid, but the dog wagged its tail and licked the crusty gash on my arm.

"Who are you?" said the boy. He wore shoes, clothes. No boils.

"Misha," I said. "Do you have water?"

The sun flashed off the steel rail.

"Where is your ear?" said the boy.

"Stawki Station."

"Where are you going?" he said.

"To the ovens."

"What ovens?"

"Where the trains go."

"Why are you going to the ovens?"

"That's where Janina is," I said. "Do you know her?"

He shook his head.

"Do you know Uri? Do you know Doctor Korczak? Do you have water?"

"Can I touch your ear?"

I said yes. He reached out. I think he touched it, but I could not feel.

He looked at me. "Are you a Jew?"

"Yes." I pulled the armband from my pocket. I slipped it onto my good arm. "See?"

"Yes."

He disappeared into the weeds with the dog. He returned with a pan of water. I drank it.

I walked on.

Day. Night. Day. Night.

I ate blackberries from thorny whips that reminded me of barbed wire. I pulled scallions from the earth. I drank from ditches, and when I bent to cup my hands in the water, the ringing pulsed in my eyes.

The steel rails flashed in the sun. I shivered as if it were winter. My wounded ear would not dry out. I awoke in the weeds. I awoke on the tracks. The steel rails wobbled away from me like silvery snakes. I was in many places, and I was not alone.

Buffo was there, smiling, waiting for me. I could smell the mint.

The blue man rode the merry-go-round to the tootling music.

I saw bodies wrapped in newspaper floating above the sidewalks.

I felt Uri smack me in the head and call me stupid.

I saw Himmler's car stop and Himmler himself get out and march right up to me and snap his heels together and salute me and say, "Hanukkah!"

I saw the orphans. They were marching down the tracks, led by Doctor Korczak. The orphans were marching and singing, their shoes all hitting the ground at once, and the oven door opened, and into the oven they went, heads held high, marching and singing.

Every day Mr. Milgrom stroked my hair.

Every day I heard Kuba laughing.

Every day I looked for Janina and every day she was not there. I was used to her constant presence, to her mimicking everything I did. I kept glancing around to see myself repeated, but there was only me.

One day when I opened my eyes, a man was standing over me.

42

The man placed his foot on my chest. "You're a Jew," he said.

"Yes," I answered. I pointed to my armband. "See?"

"What are you doing here?"

"I'm following the train. Janina. I'm going to the ovens."

"What ovens?"

"The ovens for the Jews. I'm a filthy son of Abraham. They forgot me. Can you take me to the ovens?"

The man spit in the weeds. "I don't know what you're talking about. You make no sense. Are you insane?"

That word was new to me. "I don't know. But I'm stupid. And tiny. And fast."

He jerked me to my feet. "Tiny is right." He tore the armband away. "What happened to your ear?"

"Uri did it. He tried to kill me, but he missed."

"Come with me," he said.

I took a step and fell back to the ground. When I awoke, I was bouncing in a cart pulled by a donkey. When it stopped, the man slung me over his shoulder and dumped me into a heap of hay in a barn. The farmer's wife came and gave me water and a carrot to eat. With water and rags she cleaned my wounded ear. Then she tied a rag around my head that covered the ear and one eye.

"Do you know Uri?" I said.

She tied another rag around my crusty arm.

"Did you see Janina?"

She touched my forehead. "You're burning. And you stink."

The farmer's wife put me in a wooden tub and scrubbed me until I screamed. She brought me clothes. She burned my old ones, with the shoe in the pocket.

The wife came every day and cleaned my ear and my arm and felt my forehead and gave me water and carrots and boiled turnips. I slept in the hay and played with the mice in the barn. One was my favorite. I shared my turnips with it. I called it Janina. I taught it to run up my arm and stand on my head. Then a cat ate it.

One day I awoke and the ringing was gone. I walked out of the barn and through the fields until I came to the tracks. A spot of white caught my eye—the armband, snagged on a thornbush. I stuffed it into my pocket.

I had been walking the tracks for a long time when the farmer stopped me.

"Where are you going?" he said.

"To the ovens."

The farmer knocked me down with a swat of his hand, and I was back in the donkey cart with a rope around my neck. I was tied to a stable post in the barn. I remembered Uri's story of my beginnings, of becoming a slave to farmers. Maybe the story wasn't made up after all. Maybe I was catching up with my life.

After some days the farmer's wife came to the barn and said, "You must not run away. There is a new law. All children must work on the farms."

"Then to the ovens?" I said.

"Yes," she said. "Then."

43

I slept in the barn, ate in the barn, worked in the barn. When I wasn't working in the barn, I worked in the fields. I hauled rocks to the donkey cart. I picked bugs from the vegetables (when I wasn't picking them from myself). I learned to milk the cow. One day the cow kicked me. I told it what happened to the cow in the ghetto. The farmer's wife—her name was Elzbieta—fed me with the pigs. The pigs' toilet was my toilet.

Every night I was tied to the stable post. Sometimes in the night, on the far side of the fields, I heard the huffing of locomotives and the clack of iron wheels. Many times I asked Elzbieta the wife, "When will the law be over? When can I go to the ovens?" "Soon," she always said. "But you must not run away. If you do, the Nazis will burn down the farm and feed us to the pigs."

So I worked and waited and talked with the donkey and the mice.

Then one day a man came in a horse and cart and said something to the farmer and went away. Later I heard the farmer shouting in the house. That night I was awakened by a voice, the wife's. "Run!" The rope around my ankle was gone. There was something under my shirt, against my skin. Bread. I ran.

The war was over. I had been on the farm for three years.

I was back to walking the tracks. This time I had company. Thousands were trudging the tracks, the roads, the fields. No Jackboots guarded them.

There were carnivals. Markets. They sprang up in fields along the railroad and were gone by next day. People sold things.

"Shoes!"

"Cigarette lighter!"

"Apples!"

Anything for money. Anything for food.

I saw a tent made from bedsheets. A man was calling: "Come in! Come in! See Herr Hitler! Come right in! Only fifty zlotys!"

I did not have even one zloty. I waited until someone was paying and slid under the bedsheet. Lying on the ground was a skeleton. Its bony feet had been stuffed into long black boots. A steel helmet swallowed half the grinning skull.

Another man called: "Ten zlotys! You won't believe your eyes!" There was no tent, only a handkerchief. A customer paid. The man stood in my way, so I could not see. He lifted the handkerchief and let it fall. The customer wanted his money back. While the two fought on the ground, I lifted the handkerchief. It was something I had never seen. Something Ferdi had said did not exist. Something Mr. Milgrom had said was like happy. It was an orange.

The hucksters fascinated me the most. I stood in front of them for hours as they ranted to the passing parades about the wonders under their tents and handkerchiefs. They never stopped. They never ran out of words. When I lay down in weeds or a barn at night, I whispered into the dark: "Come and look! You won't believe your eyes!"

I dreamed of bodyless Jackboots tramping the earth. I dreamed of burning cows. I dreamed the stone angel looked down on me and said, "I am nobody."

I walked the tracks and roads. I offered my services to farmers for food and a bed of straw in the barn. When there was no work, I took my food from wherever I could find it. I drank my water from bomb craters.

I rode on trains. So did many others. I rode on boxcars and cinder cars and tankers. I rode a thousand trains. None ever took me to Janina. Or to a candy mountain.

Somewhere along the way I heard the story of Hansel and Gretel, and I knew that the end was not true, that the witch did not die in the oven.

One day I found myself back in the city of Warsaw.

The bomb craters were gone. There was still rubble. Trucks and carts were hauling it away. I thought I heard a machine gun. I ducked into a doorway. It was a jackhammer. I saw people slumped in alleyways, but they were not covered in newspaper. They were sleeping for real.

I found the ghetto. The wall was gone. I walked right in. I looked for Niska Street. I could not find it. I could not find our house. Or the orphans' house. Or Olek hanging. Or the rug we slept under. There was rubble and there was nothing. Even the flies were gone.

On the trains I had heard about the revolt. Until then, I had thought I was the last one out of the ghetto. I did not know forty thousand people were still there. The following spring, as I hauled the farmer's rocks, the Jews turned on the Jackboots with stolen guns and bottle bombs. But the Jackboots were too many, with their tanks and flamethrowers, and the revolt was over by May and the people were herded to the last of the trains and the ghetto was no more.

Standing in the silent dust, I understood at last what Uri had done and what he had saved me from. I understood that the Uri I knew—the real Uri—was not the one the Nazis knew. I smiled to think of him on the last day, once again in his own clothes, shaking his fist at the oncoming tanks, his red hair flaring, invisible no more, calling all the world's attention to himself.

After I walked out of the ghetto that was no longer there, I wandered the streets of the city. I stole my food.

One day, in a crowd on a sidewalk, I caught a whiff of mint. I stopped, looked about, ran back the other way. I stared into faces. I sniffed. There it was again: *mint*. A man's mouth was working, a fleck of green on his lip. A gristly, bony man. White whiskers. Sunken eyes. Ragged clothes. Bare feet so dirty I thought at first he wore shoes or socks. No club. No fat belly.

I planted myself in front of him. He stopped.

"Fatman."

His head didn't move. His eyes sagged down to me.

I tugged on his rags. *"Fatman."*

His eyes were dead.

"Fatman, it's me. Misha. Me and Janina. Remember?"

He did not hear.

I shook him. "Fatman! Buffo! You hate me. You want to kill me. Here I am. Here"—I took his hand and put it on my head—"kill me."

His hand slid off my head and flopped to his side.

I punched him in his bony stomach. "Fatman! Look!" I pulled from my pocket something I had been carrying all this time: the armband, once blue and white, now mostly black. I rolled it up my sleeve. "Look, Fatman! I'm a Jew. You have to kill me. Look!"

But he would not look. He shuffled into me, almost knocking me down, and shuffled away. I watched until he was lost in the crowd. I took off the armband and let it fall to the sidewalk.

44

The world was returning to normal, but for me there was no normal to return to. Normal for me was stolen bread and ditch water. Little by little I learned about forks and money and toothpaste and toilets.

Back in the countryside, I did what I did best. I stole. I snatched everything I could carry. I became my own donkey. I pulled a little cart everywhere I went, and wherever I stopped I became a carnival.

I was so good at stealing, people saw things in my cart that they found nowhere else. And I was cheap. What did I know of prices? By the end of a day my pocket was only a little less empty than my wagon.

But who cared, for I had discovered my voice. I became a huckster like the ones that had fascinated me. "Ho! Bread for sale! Apples! Shoes! Cigarettes! Ladies' undergarments! Come and see! Amazing bargains!"

For me, it was more about talking than about selling. There had been a few word bursts during and before the ghetto, but up until the end of the war, I had probably not spoken two thousand words in my life. Now you could not shut me up. If my cart was empty, I kept on hawking just to hear myself talk. I wallowed in words. There was no end to them. They were free for the taking. No one ever chased me down a road yelling, "Stop! Thief! He stole my word!"

* * *

Time went by. I talked enough and stole enough and sold enough to buy a steamship ticket, and I joined the multitudes going to America.

The immigration officer said, "What is your name?" "Misha Milgrom," I said. "What's a Misha?" he said. "Your name is Jack."

I became Jack Milgrom.

I learned English. I went on talking. In America that means I was a salesman.

No one hired me to sell the best products. The problems were my size (I had stopped growing at five feet, one inch), my accent, and my missing ear, which now looked like a clump of cauliflower. I couldn't blame them. Who would let such a galoot in the door? "Good day, madam. Can I interest you in a nice vacuum cleaner?" Forget it.

Then I got my big break. I was hired to sell a miracle vegetable chopper on the boardwalk in Atlantic City, New Jersey. I was given a table and a pile of cucumbers. Ten o'clock in the morning. People gathered in front of me. I began describing the wonders of the miracle chopper. Somebody called, "Wha'd ya do, chop yer ear off?" Before I was half through my spiel, the last person was walking away. I felt desperate. "Wait!" I called. My mouth took over. "There's something I have to tell you. Doctor Korczak was right. There *was* a cow. And it burned like a marshmallow!"

The people stopped and turned. They were thinking: *What's he talking about? What's that have to do with the miracle chopper?*

Who cared, as long as I was talking?

"Himmler looked like my uncle Shepsel. My uncle Shepsel looked like a chicken. . . .

"You want to know what rat tastes like? Rat tastes like mouse. . . .

"I'm going to warn you one last time: Do *not* take the horse from the merry-go-round. . . ."

I told them everything—except for Janina—all that I had seen, all that I was. The boardwalkers streamed by in both directions. Stopped to listen: three or four. Miracle choppers sold: zero. I was fired at the end of the day.

But I had found something.

Next day I was back on the boardwalk. No cucumbers, no choppers, just me, standing near Steel Pier spouting off. Then one day I took the bus west to Philadelphia. To earn money for cheap beds in cheap places, I handed out circulars and swept gas stations and shucked oysters, but my real job was running my mouth. If you walked the streets of Philadelphia in those days, you probably heard me. Fifteenth and Market. Broad and Chestnut. You heard me and you turned, and as soon as you realized I was spouting nonsense, you turned away and walked on, muttering to your friend, "Another nutcake."

It was on a corner that I met my wife. Thirteenth and Market. A cold day in November. She stopped and listened. That was rare enough. Five minutes later she was still there. That was unheard of. Then she left. But she came back with a bag of roasted chestnuts from a street vendor. She offered me one. Her name was Vivian.

She came back every day, staying longer and longer, bringing me hot chestnuts. She lured me away from the street corner—lunch at Horn & Hardart, walks in Rittenhouse Square, card games in her ground-floor apartment.

Always I went on talking, telling my stories. Vivian became my street corner. Vivian was a normal, sensible person, but I think at that time she must have gone a little cuckoo. Maybe my words dazzled her. Maybe she saw me as a needy refugee from the war or an exotic artifact of history. In any case, one day out of the blue, she blurted, "Okay, I'll marry you," and I thought, *Did I ask?*

The marriage lasted five months. Vivian quickly found out that living with me was different from playing cards with me.

When caroling children came at Christmastime, I slammed the door in their faces.

When I saw a copy of *Hansel and Gretel* in a bookstore window, I went in and grabbed it and ripped it to shreds, and Vivian had to pay for it.

In the shower I sometimes turned on the cold water, but I could never stand it until I became blue.

I snatched apples from fruit stands.

I did strange things at parades.

I laughed in the wrong places.

I heard flies: "Remember Warsaw? What a feast! We were so full of crap we couldn't take off!"

I cried for no reason.

In the night the colossal black flame-throwing Jackboots tramped through my dreams.

Finally, Vivian had enough. As she was leaving, I stared at her stomach. "Are you pregnant?" I said.

"Good-bye," she said.

She closed the door, and I went back to the street corners. Remember the day you were hurrying by with your briefcase or shopping bag? Heading for the parking lot? The one-eared, pint-size Looney Tune ranting at you? That was me, flapping day after day about Olek and Uri and Himmler the chicken and Kuba the clown and the crows and black pearls and my yellow stone and the food that flew over the wall and the flaming, flying cow and the orphans marching and singing and the man who scrubbed the sidewalk with his beard and Buffo's belly and Doctor Korczak's cozy goatee and the ladies with white gloves and cameras and Greta the horse that never was—they were all a jumble in my head. What a mess they must have been coming out of my mouth.

And you? You were the thing that gave me shape. "But I wasn't even listening," you say. "I don't even remember you." Don't feel bad. The important thing was not that you listened, but that I talked. I can see that now. I was born into craziness. When the whole world turned crazy, I was ready for it. That's how I survived. And when the craziness was over, where did that leave me? On the street corner, that's where, running my mouth, spilling myself. And I needed you there. You were the bottle I poured myself into.

I branched out. I went to nearby towns that had never seen a street corner talker. Norristown. Conshohocken. Glenside.

The years, the words, went by.

Then one day in Philadelphia, in the shadow of City Hall, two women stopped and listened. They looked to be in their seventies. They wore wide hats that shaded their faces like little parasols. After a while one of them reached out her hand and cupped my ear clump. She smiled and nodded and said, "We hear you. It's enough. It's over." And they walked on, and I went another way, and I never took to another street corner.

When my daughter found me, I was stocking shelves in a Bag 'n Go market.

45

TODAY

"Poppynoodle! *Poppynoodle!*"

My granddaughter screams from another room. I get up from my easy chair and go see what it is this time.

"Look at me!"

I'm looking. She thinks she is standing on her head, but the toes of her pink sneakers never leave the floor. And I am once again reminded of the girl whose name she carries.

Janina.

I was putting up soup cans in aisle 4 when I heard the voice behind me.

"Mr. Milgrom?"

I turned. It was a young woman in a light blue skirt and windbreaker, dark brown hair. She was holding the hand of a little girl. The little girl looked up at me with huge, unblinking eyes.

"Daddy?" said the young woman.

I stared.

"I'm Katherine. Your daughter. I've been looking for you forever." She shifted the little girl to stand in front of her. "This is my daughter, Wendy. Your granddaughter."

"I'm four," said the little girl. "What happened to your ear?"

"Wendy," said her mother.

A distant voice that only I could hear replied: *It was shot twice. First by a Jackboot, then by Uri.*

"Did you know you're my grandfather?"

I still could not speak.

"Well, you are," she said. "Shake." She held out her hand. I held out mine. She took it and gave it one hard shake. "Please ta meetcha."

I looked at her mother.

"You didn't know about me, did you?" she said.

"I wa——" I cleared my throat. "I wasn't sure."

Her smile was radiant. "Well, I'm here. I'm twenty-five years old. I know about you from Mother. For four years now, I've been saving something for you."

I hesitated. "Yes?"

"Wendy's middle name. I left it blank. I knew someday I would find you. She's been waiting four years for a middle name. I want you to give it to her."

"Janina," I said.

My daughter's laughter rang throughout the market. "I thought you'd at least take a minute to think about it." She took the little girl's face in her hand and turned it toward herself. She nodded. "Wendy Janina. So it is."

The little girl clapped. She twirled about. "Wendy Janina! Wendy Janina!"

"We live in Elkins Park," said Katherine. "We have a spare room. You can have your own bathroom."

I dropped my apron in aisle 4. They took me home.

*   *   *

Wendy Janina tries to improve her headstand. She pushes off from her toes a little too hard, which sends her tiny body sailing past a headstand and into a backflop onto the hard floor. I wince at the thump. From the floor her eyes cast about until they find me. Her lower lip sticks out. She is deciding whether or not to cry. Secretly, I almost hope she does. I would like to be the grandfather who stops her tears.

I hold out my arms. She gets up and comes to me. I lift her to my lap. She puts her head on my chest. She doesn't cry, but it's enough.

I would like to stay this way for a year, or ten, but she leaps from my lap and pipes, "Outside!" She grabs my finger and pulls me out to the deck.

"I'll sit here," I say. I settle into the rocking chair.

"Watch me!" she says, and runs to the swing set.

I watch. She swings back and forth. The maple tree behind her is a brilliant orange. The year is gorgeous in its dying. The milkweed pods are bursting.

The milkweed does not change colors. The milkweed is as green in October as in July.

When I said one day to my daughter, Katherine, "Drive around, out of town," and I brought along a trowel and a bucket, she did not ask why. When I said, "Stop here," and dug it up, she said only, "Milkweed, right?"

I nodded.

She did not object when I planted it at the end of the yard, away from the maple. Angel plants must have sun.

My daughter does not pester me with questions. She knows

207

everything that I told her mother, which means everything but Janina. All those years of talking, all those street corners—I kept my sister to myself.

One time Katherine said to me, "Are you ever going to tell me why you named her Janina?"

"Someday," I said.

At last Wendy Janina tires of the swing. Or maybe she just wants a ride on the rocker, me doing the work. She plops down on my lap. "Rock, Poppynoodle!"

I rock. I smile. I close my eyes. I think of all the voices that have told me who I have been, the names I've had. Call me thief. Call me stupid. Call me Gypsy. Call me Jew. Call me one-eared Jack. I don't care. Empty-handed victims once told me who I was. Then Uri told me. Then an armband. Then an immigration officer. And now this little girl in my lap, this little girl whose call silences the tramping Jackboots. Her voice will be the last. I was. Now I am. I am . . . Poppynoodle.

JERRY SPINELLI

MILKWEED

A NOVEL

A READER'S GUIDE

QUESTIONS FOR DISCUSSION

1. Identity is a key theme in *Milkweed*. Discuss what Misha Pilsudski means when he says, "And so, thanks to Uri, in a cellar beneath a barbershop somewhere in Warsaw, Poland, in autumn of the year nineteen thirty-nine, I was born, you might say" (p. 31). How does the made-up story of Misha's life become so important to him? How does his identity change throughout the novel? What gives him a true identity at the end of the book? Discuss Uncle Shepsel's efforts to renounce his identity as a Jew. How are these efforts related to survival?

2. Uri is described as "fearless on the streets" (p. 80). What does he teach Misha about fear? Janina has led a privileged life and has not had to deal with fear before her family is moved to the ghetto. Discuss how Misha helps her cope with her new life. How does fear eventually kill Mrs. Milgrom? At what point in the novel does Misha display the most fear? How does he deal with it?

3. Uri advises Misha and the other homeless boys that one important survival skill is remaining invisible. Why does Misha have a difficult time remaining invisible? What other survival skills do the boys employ? What does Misha teach the Milgroms about survival? What poses the greatest threat to the survival of the Jews in the ghetto?

4. How does Misha's relationship with the Milgroms change throughout the novel? At what point does Mr. Milgrom invite him to become a part of the family? Why are Uncle Shepsel and Mrs. Milgrom so reluctant to accept Misha? Discuss how Misha's desire for family comes full circle by the end of the book.

5. In this novel about the horror and destruction of the Holocaust, Jerry Spinelli includes a number of recurring images of innocence and childhood. He also creates a main character who is young and naïve. What is the effect of this blending of the horrific and the innocent? What is the importance of the carousel horses, the angels, and Janina's shiny black shoes? Why does Misha say, "We couldn't eat merry-go-round horses and stone angels" (p. 138)? How do Misha's childlike feelings and ideas about the Jackboots, their "parades," and the war change?

6. Although they are hungry and grieving, the Milgroms still celebrate Hanukkah—even after their silver menorah has been stolen. What is the importance of their faith and hope in the midst of devastation? How does Misha feel when he is included in the celebration? The first time Misha hears the word "happy" is when Mr. Milgrom uses it to describe Hanukkah and being proud of their Jewish heritage (p. 157)—why is this important? Why does Misha give up the idea that he is a Gypsy in favor of being a Jew?

7. Discuss the qualities of true friendship. Talk about the friendship that develops between Misha and Janina. Why is Misha such a good friend to the orphans? Why does Dr. Korczak, the head of the orphanage, call Misha a "foolish, good-hearted boy" (p. 64)?

8. When Misha comes to the United States, he shares on the street corner his memories of his life in Poland. He says that running is his first memory (p. 1). What might he say is his last memory? Misha doesn't tell his family about Janina, but he pays tribute to her memory by naming his granddaughter for her. Discuss why he wants to keep the memory of Janina to himself.

QUESTIONS FOR DISCUSSION

9. On page 196, Misha says, "Somewhere along the way I heard the story of Hansel and Gretel, and I knew that the end was not true, that the witch did not die in the oven." When he is older and moves to America, Misha sees a copy of *Hansel and Gretel* in a bookstore and "grab[s] it and rip[s] it to shreds" (p. 202). Think about the story of Hansel and Gretel. How does this story—which most people see as a simple fairy tale—emphasize the horror of the Holocaust for Misha? How are Misha and Janina like Hansel and Gretel? Do you think Misha's wife, Vivian, understands why he rips up the book?

10. The first sentence of *Milkweed* is "I am running" (p. 1). Later, Uri warns Misha to run from the ghetto to escape the deportation: "'Get out. Run. Don't stop running'" (p. 169). On page 180, Mr. Milgrom tells Misha to take Janina to the other side of the wall and run away: "'Do not bring back food tonight. Do not return. Run. *Run.*'" Running plays an important role in *Milkweed*. How does it shape Misha's life and identity? Do you think Misha is able to stop running at the end of the novel?

11. Think about the title—where does milkweed appear in this novel? What does it mean to Misha and Janina when they're in the ghetto? What does milkweed mean to Misha at the end of the novel when he plants it at the end of his yard? How does it preserve his memories of Poland?

A CONVERSATION WITH

JERRY SPINELLI

Q: How was writing *Milkweed*—your first historical novel— different from writing your other novels?
A: Research is what made it different from my other books. I usually do little research, but there was no avoiding it here. I made my bookseller happy by buying a load of books. I read parts of all of them for the next four or five months, then started writing.

Q: Would you mind telling us about the two people you named in your *Milkweed* dedication?
A: Bill Bryzgornia, a lifelong friend of mine, died shortly before the book came out. He was of Polish descent. He is mentioned briefly in my autobiography, *Knots in My Yo-yo String*.

Masha Bruskina is the name of a young woman who was publicly hanged by the Nazis as a warning and an example to partisan opponents of the occupying forces. I had seen the picture of her execution in a number of books over the years.

Q: How much of Misha's character and situation is based on history, on reality? What about the other characters?
A: Many of the events and details of the story are true. For the most part, I made up the characters. There were, in fact, orphans who had no memory of mother or father and who, it seemed, simply materialized on the streets of war-torn Europe.

Q: Why did you decide to show the reader what happens to Misha when he grows up rather than ending *Milkweed* with him still a child?
A: Because I wasn't telling the story of the war; I was telling the story of Misha.

Q: How did you decide on the names of the characters?
A: As always, I chose them because they sounded right for the story, the time, the place. In a few cases, I actually changed names on the advice of a few helpful prepublication readers who knew 1940s Poland better than I.

Q: Do you have any favorite historical novels?
A: *Johnny Tremain.*

Q: When did you realize you wanted to be a writer?
A: Eleventh grade, around the time a poem of mine about a football game was published in the local newspaper. I guess it was largely a matter of timing. I was sixteen. My dream of becoming a major-league baseball player was fading. The imperative to find my course in life was upon me. I was shopping around for who I wanted to be. And here this writing thing seemed to reach down and pluck me out of the crowd. I mean, it wasn't forced, it wasn't planned. Nobody assigned me to write a poem after the game. I didn't try to get it published. I didn't seek the resulting notoriety. All this pretty much just happened to me. What I did was just apply a little common sense: I like to write, I seem to be pretty good at it, people seem to like what I write (admittedly a lot to conclude from a single poem)—ergo, I'll be a writer. Simple!

Q: If you could have dinner with anyone in the world, whom would you choose, and why?

A: Tie: Loren Eiseley, the anthropologist and poet/essayist, and Sonny Liston, former heavyweight champ.

Loren Eiseley because he's often the answer when I'm asked, "Who is your favorite writer?" It's incredible that he wrote so well, considering that he was a scientist. I love his insights and perspectives on humankind and the universe. . . .

On the way home to St. Louis after winning the heavyweight title, Sonny Liston looked forward to a hero's welcome, looked forward to receiving affection from the people who had regarded him as a hoodlum and a monster. When he stepped off the plane, not a soul was there to greet him. It broke his heart. I'd like to ask him about that day. I'd like to dump a teacup of confetti on his head.

Q: What do you consider the most rewarding part of writing books for young people?

A: Feedback from readers. The most common kind, of course, is fan mail. I'm proud to say that one particularly nice letter was submitted by the reader/writer to a fan mail contest run by the Library of Congress, and it won. It was about *Crash*. Some of the most heartwarming reports I get are from teachers and librarians whom I meet personally at conferences and book signings. When a teacher with tears in her eyes tells how a book "saved" a student of hers, I know I'm in the right business. I remember a letter from a teacher in Georgia. She told me the kids in her class had a choice one day: they could go eat lunch, or they could continue to listen to my book. Every one stayed for the book.

A CONVERSATION WITH JERRY SPINELLI

Q: Do you ever use suggestions from readers in new books?
A: I tell readers that if I use an idea of theirs in a book, I'll give them credit in the acknowledgments. This paid off for one student, who gave me the idea for one of the School Daze books: *Who Ran My Underwear Up the Flagpole?*

Q: What advice do you have for young writers?
A: For me, there are many little rules, all superseded by one Golden Rule: Write what you *care* about.

CLAY
David Almond
978-0-440-42013-2
A gifted sculptor, Stephen can form lifelike figures out of clay. One day, Davie helps Stephen bring a man-sized sculpture to life—and Clay is born. But as Clay turns from childlike to monstrous, Davie is the only one with the power to set him—and himself—free.

COUNTING STARS
David Almond
978-0-440-41826-9
With stories that shimmer and vibrate in the bright heat of memory, David Almond creates a glowing mosaic of his life growing up in a large, loving Catholic family in northeastern England.

HEAVEN EYES
David Almond
978-0-440-22910-0
Erin Law and her friends in the orphanage are labeled Damaged Children. They run away one night, traveling downriver on a raft. What they find on their journey is stranger than you can imagine.

KIT'S WILDERNESS
David Almond
978-0-440-41605-0
Kit Watson and John Askew look for the childhood ghosts of their long-gone ancestors in the mines of Stoneygate.

BEFORE WE WERE FREE
Julia Alvarez
978-0-440-23784-6
Under a dictatorship in the Dominican Republic in 1960, young Anita lives through a fight for freedom that changes her world forever.

FINDING MIRACLES
Julia Alvarez
978-0-553-49406-8
Fifteen-year-old Milly has never told anyone in her small Vermont town that she's adopted. But when Pablo, a refugee from Milly's birth country, transfers to her school, she is forced to confront her true identity.

FORGOTTEN FIRE
Adam Bagdasarian
978-0-440-22917-9
In 1915, Vahan Kenderian is living a life of privilege when his world is shattered by the Turkish-Armenian war.

COLIBRÍ
Ann Cameron
978-0-440-42052-1
At age four, Colibrí was kidnapped from her parents in Guatemala City, and ever since then she's traveled with Uncle, who believes Colibrí will lead him to treasure. Danger mounts as Uncle grows desperate for his fortune—and as Colibrí grows daring in seeking her freedom.

THE CHOCOLATE WAR
Robert Cormier
978-0-375-82987-1
Jerry Renault dares to disturb the universe in this groundbreaking and now classic novel, an unflinching portrait of corruption and cruelty in a boys' prep school.

THE RAG AND BONE SHOP
Robert Cormier
978-0-440-22971-1
A seven-year-old girl is brutally murdered. A twelve-year-old boy named Jason was the last person to see her alive—except, of course, for the killer. Unless *Jason* is the killer.

BUD, NOT BUDDY
Christopher Paul Curtis
978-0-553-49410-5
Ten-year-old Bud's momma never told him who his father was, but she left a clue: flyers advertising Herman E. Calloway and his famous band. Bud's got an idea that those flyers will lead him to his father. Once he decides to hit the road and find this mystery man, nothing can stop him.

THE WATSONS GO TO BIRMINGHAM—1963
Christopher Paul Curtis
978-0-440-41412-4
Nine-year-old Kenny tells hilarious stories about his family, the Weird

Watsons of Flint, Michigan. When Kenny's thirteen-year-old brother, Byron, gets to be too much trouble, they head south to Birmingham to visit Grandma, the one person who can shape him up. And they happen to be in Birmingham when Grandma's church is blown up.

FAREWELL TO MANZANAR
Jeanne Wakatsuki Houston and James D. Houston
978-0-553-27258-1
The true story of one spirited Japanese American family's efforts to survive the indignities of forced detention during World War II . . . and of a native-born American child who discovered what it was like to grow up behind barbed wire in the United States.

GHOST BOY
Iain Lawrence
978-0-440-41668-5
Fourteen-year-old Harold Kline is an albino—an outcast. When the circus comes to town, Harold runs off to join it in hopes of discovering who he is and what he wants in life. Is he a circus freak or just a normal guy?

LORD OF THE NUTCRACKER MEN
Iain Lawrence
978-0-440-41812-2
Johnny eagerly plays at war with the army of nutcracker soldiers his toy-maker father whittles for him. But in 1914, Germany looms as the real enemy of Europe, and Johnny's father enlists to fight in France. As letters arrive for Johnny from the front, they reveal the ugly realities of combat—and Johnny fears that the mock battles he stages in his back-yard foretell his father's fate.

THE GIVER
Lois Lowry
978-0-385-73255-0
Jonas's world is perfect. Everything is under control. There is no war or fear or pain. There are no choices, until Jonas is given an opportunity that will change his world forever.

ACCELERATION
Graham McNamee
978-0-440-23836-2
It's a hot, hot summer, and in the depths of the Toronto Transit

Authority's Lost and Found, seventeen-year-old Duncan is cataloging lost things and sifting through accumulated junk. Then he finds a little leather book. It's a diary filled with the dark and dirty secrets of a twisted mind, a serial killer stalking his prey in the subway. And Duncan can't make himself stop reading.

IN MY HANDS: MEMORIES OF A HOLOCAUST RESCUER
by Irene Gut Opdyke with Jennifer Armstrong
978-0-553-49411-2

The remarkable true story of a powerless young woman who defied the Nazis. When forced to work in a German officers' dining hall, Irene eavesdropped on the Nazis' plans and passed information to Jews in the ghetto. She smuggled people from the work camp into the forest. And when she was made the housekeeper of a Nazi major, she hid twelve Jews in the basement of his home until the Germans' defeat.

CUBA 15
Nancy Osa
978-0-385-73233-8

Violet Paz's upcoming *quinceañero,* a girl's traditional fifteenth-birthday coming-of-age ceremony, awakens her interest in her Cuban roots—and sparks a fire of conflicting feelings about Cuba within her family.

HOLES
Louis Sachar
978-0-440-22859-2

Stanley has been unjustly sent to a boys' detention center, Camp Green Lake. But there's more than character improvement going on at the camp—the warden is looking for something.

EYES OF THE EMPEROR
Graham Salisbury
978-0-440-22956-8

Eddy Okana lies about his age and joins the army in his hometown, Honolulu, only weeks before the Japanese bomb Pearl Harbor. Suddenly, Americans see him as the enemy. Even the U.S. Army doubts the loyalty of Japanese American enlisted men. Then Eddy and a small band of Japanese American soldiers are sent on a secret mission to a small island. They are given a special job, one that only they can do.

LIZZIE BRIGHT AND THE BUCKMINSTER BOY
Gary D. Schmidt
978-0-375-84169-9
Turner Buckminster is miserable about being the son of the new minister in a small Maine town. It feels as if everyone is watching his every move—and every mistake he makes. One huge mistake is his forbidden friendship with lively Lizzie Bright Griffin, an African American girl from a poor community founded by former slaves.

STARGIRL
Jerry Spinelli
978-0-440-41677-7
Stargirl. From the day she arrives at quiet Mica High in a burst of color and sound, the hallways hum with the murmur of "Stargirl, Stargirl." The students are enchanted. Then they turn on her.

SHABANU: DAUGHTER OF THE WIND
Suzanne Fisher Staples
978-0-440-23856-0
Life is both sweet and cruel to strong-willed young Shabanu, whose home is the windswept Cholistan Desert of Pakistan. She must reconcile her duty to her family and the stirrings of her own heart in this Newbery Honor–winning modern-day classic.

THE BOOK THIEF
Markus Zusak
978-0-375-84220-7
Trying to make sense of the horrors of World War II, Death tells the story of Liesel Meminger—a German girl whose book-stealing and storytelling talents sustain her foster family and the Jewish man they are hiding in their basement, along with their neighbors. This is an unforgettable story about the power of words and the ability of books to feed the soul.

Also available
Stargirl
by Jerry Spinelli

A *New York Times* Bestseller
A *Parents' Choice Gold Award* Winner
A *Publishers Weekly* Best Book of the Year
An ALA Top Ten Best Book for Young Adults
A *Book Sense National* Bestseller
A *Publishers Weekly* Bestseller

★ "A magical and heartbreaking tale."
—*Kirkus Reviews*, Starred

"Spinelli has produced a poetic allegorical tale about the
magnificence and rarity of true nonconformity."
—*The New York Times*

★ "Part fairy godmother, part outcast,
part dream-come-true, [Stargirl] possesses many of the
mythical qualities of Maniac Magee."
—*Publishers Weekly*, Starred

"Stargirl is luminescent. . . . This book resonates
long after the cover is closed."
—*The Detroit News and Free Press*

Also available
Love, Stargirl

by Jerry Spinelli

Also available
Crash
by Jerry Spinelli

Hut! Hut! Hut!

Everybody knows Crash Coogan, seventh-grade football sensation. He's been mowing down everything in his path since the time he could walk—and Penn Webb, his dweeby, vegetable-eating neighbor, is his favorite target. After all, Webb's not just a nerd, he's a cheerleader, too.

Crash and his best buddy, Mike, can't think of anything more hilarious than making Webb's life miserable. But Crash starts to realize that Webb has something he may never gain, no matter how many touchdowns he scores. And when Mike takes a prank too far, maybe even for Crash, the football star has to choose which side he's really on.

"Spinelli packs a powerful moral wallop, leaving it to
the pitch-perfect narration to drive home his point."
—*Publishers Weekly*

★ "Readers will devour this humorous glimpse of what jocks
are made of." —*School Library Journal*, Starred

"Great fun to read." —*The Horn Book Magazine*

today i will

A YEAR *of* QUOTES, NOTES, *and* PROMISES *to* MYSELF

by EILEEN & JERRY SPINELLI

TODAY I will welcome surprises.

TODAY I will do one small, brave thing.

TODAY I will be my own best self.

today i will.

Inspired by 366 quotes from children's literature, award-winning authors Eileen and Jerry Spinelli offer insight and reassuring advice for every day of the year. Perfect for backpacks and bedsides, this cozy volume features black-and-white spot art throughout and provides year-round "page a day" inspiration for kids (and adults) everywhere.